True Story
Lucius, or the Ass

T0347047

True Story
Lucius, or the Ass

Lucian

Translated by Paul Turner

Illustrated by
Hellmuth Weissenborn

ALMA CLASSICS

ALMA CLASSICS
an imprint of

ALMA BOOKS LTD
3 Castle Yard
Richmond
Surrey TW10 6TF
United Kingdom
www.almaclassics.com

True Story and *Lucius, or the Ass* first published by John Calder
(Publishers) Ltd in 1958
This edition first published by Alma Classics in 2018
Translation and introduction © Alma Books, 1958, 2018

Cover design by Will Dady

Printed and bound in Great Britain by CPI Group (UK) Ltd, CR0 4YY

ISBN: 978-1-84749-749-9

All the pictures in this volume are reprinted with permission or presumed
to be in the public domain. Every effort has been made to ascertain and
acknowledge their copyright status, but should there have been any
unwitting oversight on our part, we would be happy to rectify the error
in subsequent printings.

All rights reserved. No part of this publication may be reproduced, stored
in or introduced into a retrieval system, or transmitted, in any form or
by any means (electronic, mechanical, photocopying, recording or otherwise), without the prior written permission of the publisher. This book is
sold subject to the condition that it shall not be resold, lent, hired out or
otherwise circulated without the express prior consent of the publisher.

Contents

INTRODUCTION

T RUE STORY IS PROBABLY the best known and
  certainly the most entertaining work of Lucian, a
Syrian who was born about 115 and died about 200 AD.
Not much is known about him, apart from what can
be deduced from his own writings, but he evidently
did a great deal of travelling, not only in "the realms
of gold", but also in Greece, Italy, France and Egypt,
where he spent the last part of his life. He was thus
able to draw on his own experience for the many real-
istic details which lend an air of verisimilitude to this
fantastic traveller's tale.

It is not known for certain who wrote *Lucius, or
The Ass*, but it has long been tentatively ascribed to
Lucian, and there seems to be no conclusive reason for
rejecting this tradition. The plot of *The Ass* was used
by Apuleius in his more famous *Golden Ass*, but here
again there is some doubt whether Apuleius borrowed
from the author of *The Ass*, or whether both writers
borrowed from a lost original, possibly written by a
man called Lucius of Patrae.

For the ordinary reader, neither of these questions is
important. All that matters is that they should realize
the difference in character, tone and intention between
the two surviving versions of the story; for though it
is fashionable for admirers of Apuleius to pour scorn
on Lucian, it is no more reasonable to do so than to

condemn, say, Virgil's treatment of the Orpheus myth in the *Georgics* merely because it is unlike M. Jean Cocteau's *Orphée*.

The main points of difference between the two Asses are these: Apuleius uses the story as a receptacle for a heterogeneous collection of anecdotes, and as a semi-allegorical vehicle for his religious ideas. *Lucius*, on the other hand, is just a well-constructed long short story designed to exploit to the utmost all the humorous and satirical possibilities of the plot, and to do nothing else. The astonishing assortment of heterogeneous material in the *Golden Ass*, combined with its greater length, has deluded critics into regarding it as a much finer work than its Greek counterpart. It is arguable, however, that though the *Golden Ass* undoubtedly expresses a very interesting personality, and though the interpolated story of Cupid and Psyche is undeniably beautiful, the less pretentious *Ass* is artistically the better production. To my temperament, it is certainly the more congenial.

For the literary historian, the chief interest of *True Story* is that it originates a genre which includes such books as *Gulliver's Travels* and *Baron Münchausen*. For me, its main attraction is that I find it extremely funny, and am perpetually astonished by the mad fertility of its invention. Reading it is rather like watching an acrobat in a modern circus, where it is no longer considered enough to swing by your teeth from a rope held by an inverted lady on a trapeze: you must at the same time play the violin, and if possible do some juggling with your feet. Lucian has much the same capacity for always going one better than my wildest expectations.

Lucius, or The Ass appeals to me not only for its impudent humour and its highly efficient narrative technique, but also for a quality which is very rare in ancient literature: a vein of sympathy for animal life. At first sight, the account of Lucius's sufferings in his donkey state may seem merely a light-hearted joke, comparable to the description of Mr Bultitude's discomfiture in *Vice Versa*, but it is impossible to read it closely without feeling that it is also a serious protest against cruelty to animals. Thus, for all its apparent cynicism, *Lucius* belongs in part to the same tradition as the Comtesse de Segur's *Memoires d'un Ane* and Anna Sewell's *Black Beauty*.

Both stories serve to illustrate the typical Lucianic attitude, which might be summed up as a refusal to be taken in by pretentious nonsense, and a determination to get as much fun as possible out of everything. No doubt Lucian's passion for debunking sometimes makes him underestimate some of the most important things in life, but his general effect is not to blunt the reader's sensibility, but to sharpen it by infecting him with some of his own *joie de vivre*. In this respect, he is strikingly unlike the general run of satirists, who tend to give the impression that life is not worth living.

My translation was mainly designed to convey the liveliness, the irreverence and the down-to-earth realism of Lucian's manner, while preventing his incidental witticisms from being lost in transit from Greek to English. With this end in view, I have allowed myself certain liberties. In order to reproduce some of his more intractable puns, I have occasionally had to make slight alterations in the sense. The most flagrant instance of this occurs in the passage where Homer is explaining the derivation of his name.

I have also allowed myself some mild anachronisms. The first of these occurs in the opening sentence of *True Story*, where I have translated "the Pillars of Hercules" as "Gibraltar". But throughout the whole story Lucian is trying, in accordance with the best traditions of science fiction, to substantiate his fantasy by reference to specific details in the world of fact. Had I used the original expression, I think it would have conveyed to the average modern reader the very opposite of what Lucian intended: a misty mythological abstraction instead of a precise geographical point.

In defence of certain other anachronistic phrases, I would argue that anachronism forms an integral part of Lucian's iconoclastic technique. He is happiest when describing revered figures of myth and poetry in terms of ordinary contemporary life; and the best way of producing this effect in a translation is probably to allow some faint echoes from the twentieth century to supplement the deliberate discords created by the second.

Finally, a classical scholar might well object to my occasional use of near-slang phrases in translating an author who is famous in his period for the comparative purity of his Greek. I would answer that translation *in toto* from one language and age to another is a complete impossibility. One can only bring out those aspects of a given work which seem most important, and ignore the rest. In this case, I felt it was more important to bring out Lucian's modernity of attitude than to attempt an exact English equivalent for his actual Greek style. As a matter of fact, the latter alternative would hardly have been practicable, for Lucian's Greek was modelled on that of writers like Plato, who lived five centuries before his time – so presumably the only way of satisfying a purist on this point would be to translate Lucian into the language of Chaucer.

P. D. L. T.
London, 1957

TRUE STORY

PREFACE

I F YOU WERE TRAINING to be an athlete, you would not spend all your time doing exercises: you would also have to learn when and how to relax, for relaxation is generally regarded as one of the most important elements in physical training. To my mind, it is equally important for intellectuals. When you have been doing a lot of serious reading, it is a good idea to give your mind a rest and so build up energy for another bout of hard work.

For this purpose the best sort of book to read is one that is not merely witty and entertaining but also has something interesting to say. I am sure you will agree that this story of mine falls into that category, for its charm consists not only in the remarkable nature of its subject matter and the beauty of its style, not only in the plausibility of its various flights of fancy, but also in its satirical intention – since every episode is a subtle parody of some fantastic "historical fact" recorded by an ancient poet, historian or philosopher.

There is no need to tell you their names, for you will recognize them soon enough, but I might just mention Ctesias of Cnidos, who made a number of statements in his history of India for which he had no evidence whatsoever, either at first or second hand. Then there was Iambulus, who told us a lot of surprising things about the Atlantic Ocean. They were obviously quite untrue, but no one could deny that they made a very good story, so hundreds of people followed his example and wrote so-called histories of their travels describing all the huge monsters, and savage tribes, and extraordinary ways of life that they had come across in foreign parts.

Of course, the real pioneer in this type of tomfoolery was Homer's Odysseus, who told Alcinous and his court an extremely tall story about bags full of wind, and one-eyed giants, and cannibals and other unpleasant characters, not to speak of many-headed monsters and magic potions that turned human beings into animals. He evidently thought the Phaeacians were fools enough to believe anything.

I do not feel particularly shocked by this kind of thing on moral grounds, for I have found that a similar disregard for truth is quite common even among professional philosophers. My chief reaction is astonishment – that anyone should tell such lies and expect to get away with it. But if other people can do it, why should not I? For I too am vain enough to wish to leave some record of myself to posterity, and as no interesting experiences have ever come my way in real life, I have nothing true to write about.

In one respect, however, I shall be a more honest liar than my predecessors, for I am telling you frankly, here and now, that I have no intention whatsoever of telling the truth. Let this voluntary confession forestall any future criticism: I am writing about things entirely outside my own experience or anyone else's – things that have no reality whatever and never could have. So mind you do not believe a word I say.

BOOK I

I ONCE SET SAIL FROM GIBRALTAR with a brisk wind
behind me and steered westward into the Atlantic. My
reason for doing so? Mere curiosity. I just felt I needed a
change, and wanted to find out what happened on the other
side of the ocean, and what sort of people lived there. With
this object in view, I had taken on board an enormous supply
of food and water, and collected fifty other young men who
felt the same way as I did to keep me company. I had also
provided all the weapons that we could possibly need, hired
the best steersman available (at an exorbitant wage) and had
our ship, which was only a light craft, specially reinforced
to withstand the stresses and strains of a long voyage.

After sailing along at a moderate speed for twenty-four hours, we were still within sight of land, but at dawn the following day the wind increased to gale force, the waves rose mountain-high, the sky grew black as night and it became impossible even to take in sail. There was nothing we could do but let her run before the wind and hope for the best.

The storm went on for seventy-nine days, but on the eightieth the sun suddenly shone through and revealed an island not far off. It was hilly and covered with trees, and now that the worst of the storm was over, the roar of the waves breaking against the shore had died down to a soft murmur. So we landed and threw ourselves down, utterly exhausted, on the sand. After all we had been through, you can imagine how long we lay there; but eventually we got up, and leaving thirty men to guard the ship, I and the other twenty went off to explore the island.

We started walking inland through the woods, and when we had gone about six hundred yards, we came across a bronze tablet with a Greek inscription on it. The letters were almost worn away, but we just managed to make out the words: "Hercules and Dionysus got this far." We also spotted a couple of footprints on a rock nearby, one about a hundred feet long, and the other, I should say, about ninety-nine. Presumably Hercules has somewhat larger feet than Dionysus.

We sank reverently to our knees and said a prayer. Then we went on a bit farther and came to a river of wine, which tasted exactly like Chianti. It was deep enough in places to float a battleship, and any doubts we might have had about the authenticity of the inscription were immediately dispelled. Dionysus had been there all right!

I was curious to know where the river came from, so I walked upstream until I arrived at the source, which was of a most unusual kind. It consisted of a group of giant vines, loaded with enormous grapes. From the root of each plant trickled sparkling drops of wine, which eventually converged to form the river. There were lots of wine-coloured fish swimming about in it, and they tasted like wine too, for we caught and ate some, and they made us extremely drunk. Needless to say, when we cut them open we found they were full of wine lees. Later, we hit on the idea of diluting them with ordinary water fish and thus reducing the alcoholic content of our food.

After lunch, we waded across the river at one of the shallower spots, and came upon some specimens of a very rare type of vine. They had good thick trunks growing out of the ground in the normal manner, but apart from that they were women, complete in every detail from the waist upwards. In fact, they were exactly like those pictures you see of Daphne being turned into a tree just as Apollo is about to catch her. From the tips of their fingers sprouted vine shoots loaded with grapes, and their hair consisted of vine leaves and tendrils.

When we went up to them, they shook us warmly by the hand and said they were delighted to see us, some saying it in Lydian, some in Hindustani, but most of them in Greek. Then they wanted us to kiss them, and every man who put his lips to theirs got very drunk and started lurching about. They would not allow us to pick their fruit, and shrieked with pain when anyone tried to do so, but they were more than willing to be deflowered, and two of the men who volunteered to oblige them found it quite impossible to withdraw from their engagements afterwards. They became literally rooted to the spot, their fingers turning into vine shoots and their hair into tendrils, and looked like having little grapes of their own at any moment.

So we left them to their fate and ran back to the ship, where we told the others what we had seen, and described the results of the experiment in cross-fertilization. Then we went off again with buckets to replenish our water supply and, while we were about it, to restock our cellar from the river. After that, we spent the night on the beach beside our ship, and next morning put to sea with a gentle breeze behind us.

About midday, when we had already lost sight of the island, we were suddenly hit by a typhoon, which whirled the ship round at an appalling speed and lifted it to a height of approximately 1,800,000 feet. While we were up there, a powerful wind caught our sails and bellied them out, so instead of falling back on to the sea, we continued to sail through the air for the next seven days – and, of course, an equal number of nights. On the eighth day we sighted what looked like a big island hanging in mid-air, white and round and brilliantly illuminated, so we steered towards it, dropped anchor and disembarked.

A brief reconnaissance was enough to tell us that the country was inhabited and under cultivation, and so long as it was light that was all we could discover about our situation; but as soon as it got dark, we noticed several other flame-coloured islands of various sizes in the vicinity, and far below us we could see a place full of towns and rivers and seas and forests and mountains, which we took to be the Earth.

We decided to do some more exploring, but we had not gone far before we were stopped and arrested by the local police. They are known in those parts as the Flying Squad, because they fly about on vultures, which they ride and control like horses. I should explain that the vultures in question are unusually large and generally have three heads. To give you some idea of their size, each of their feathers is considerably longer and thicker than the mast of a fairly large merchant ship.

Now, one of the Flying Squad's duties is to fly about the country looking for undesirable aliens, and, if it sees any, to take them before the King. So that is what they did with us.

One glance at our clothes was enough to tell the King our nationality.

"Why, you're Greek, aren't you?" he said.

"We certainly are," I replied.

"Then how on earth did you get here?" he asked. "How did you manage to come all that way through the air?" So I told him the whole story, after which he told us his. It turned out that he came from Greece too, and was called Endymion. For some reason or other he had been whisked up here in his sleep and made king of the country, which was, he informed us, the Moon.

"But don't you worry," he went on. "I'll see you have everything you need. And if I win this war with Phaethon, you can settle down here quite comfortably for the rest of your lives."

"What's the war about?" I asked.

"Oh, it's been going on for ages," he answered. "Phaethon's my opposite number on the Sun, you know. It all started like this. I thought it would be a good idea to collect some of the poorer members of the community and send them off to form a colony on Lucifer, for it's completely uninhabited. Phaethon got jealous and dispatched a contingent of airborne troops, mounted on flying ants, to intercept us when we were halfway there. We were hopelessly outnumbered and had to retreat, but now I'm going to have another shot at founding that colony, this time with full military support. If you'd care to join the expedition, I'd be only too glad to supply you with vultures from the royal stables, and all other necessary equipment. We start first thing tomorrow morning."

"Thanks very much," I said. "We'd love to come."

So he gave us an excellent meal and put us up for the night, and early next morning assembled all his troops in battle formation, for the enemy were reported to be not far off. The expeditionary force numbered a hundred thousand, exclusive of transport, engineers, infantry, and foreign auxiliaries, eighty thousand being mounted on vultures, and the other twenty on saladfowls. Saladfowls, incidentally, are like very large birds, except that they are fledged with vegetables instead of feathers and have wings composed of enormous lettuce leaves.

The main force was supported by a battery of peashooters and a corps of garlic-gassers, and also by a large contingent of allies from the Great Bear, consisting of thirty thousand flea-shooters and fifty thousand windjammers. Flea-shooters are archers mounted on fleas – hence their name – the fleas in question being approximately twelve times the size of elephants. Windjammers are also airborne troops, but they are not mounted on anything, nor do they have any wings of their own. Their method of propulsion is as follows: they wear extremely long nightshirts, which belly out like sails in the wind and send them scudding along like miniature ships through the air. Needless to say, their equipment is usually very light.

In addition to all these, seventy thousand sparrow-balls and fifty thousand crane cavalry were supposed to be arriving from the stars that shine over Cappadocia, but I did not see any of them, for they never turned up. In the circumstances, I shall not attempt to describe what they were like – though I heard some stories about them which were really quite incredible.

All Endymion's troops wore the same type of equipment. Their helmets were made of beans, which grow very large and tough up there, and their bodies were protected by lupin seed pods, stitched together to form a sort of armour-plate, for on the Moon these pods are composed of a horny substance which is practically impenetrable. As for their shields and swords, they were of the normal Greek pattern.

Our battle formation was as follows. On the right wing were the troops mounted on vultures; among them was the King, surrounded by the pick of his fighting men, which included us. On the left wing were the troops mounted on saladfowls, and in the centre were the various allied contingents.

The infantry numbered approximately sixty million, and special steps had to be taken before they could be suitably deployed. There are, you must understand, large numbers of spiders on the Moon, each considerably larger than the average island in the Archipelago, and their services were requisitioned to construct a continuous cobweb between the Moon and Lucifer. As soon as the job had been done and the infantry had thus been placed on a firm footing, Nycterion, the third son of Eudianax, led them out on to the field of battle.

On the enemy's left wing was stationed the Royal Ant Force, with Phaethon himself among them. These creatures looked exactly like ordinary flying ants, except for their enormous size, being anything up to two hundred feet long. They carried armed men on their backs, but with their huge antennae they did just as much of the fighting as their riders. They were believed to number about fifty thousand.

On the right wing were placed an equal number of gnat-shooters, who were archers mounted on giant gnats. Behind them was a body of mercenaries from outer space. These were only light-armed infantry, but were very effective long-range fighters, for they bombarded us with colossal radishes, which inflicted foul-smelling wounds and caused instantaneous death. The explanation was said to be that the projectiles were smeared with a powerful poison.

Next to the mercenaries were about ten thousand mushroom commandos – heavy-armed troops trained for hand-to-hand combat who used mushrooms as shields and asparagus stalks as spears; and next to them again were five thousand bow-wows from Sirius. These were dog-faced human beings mounted on flying chestnuts.

It was reported that Phaethon too had been let down by some of his allies, for an army of slingers was supposed to be coming from the Milky Way, and the cloud-centaurs had also promised their support. But the latter arrived too late for the battle (though far too soon for my comfort, I may add) and the slingers never turned up at all. Phaethon, I heard, was so cross about it that he went and burned their milk for them shortly afterwards.

Eventually the signal flags went up, there was a loud braying of donkeys on both sides – for donkeys are employed as trumpeters up there – and the battle began. The enemy's left wing immediately turned tail and fled, long before our vulture-riders had got anywhere near them, so we set off in pursuit and killed as many as we could. Their right wing, however, managed to break through our left one, and the gnat-shooters came pouring through the gap until they were stopped by our infantry, who promptly made a counter-attack and forced them to retreat. Finally, when they realized that their left wing had already been beaten, the retreat became an absolute rout. We took vast numbers of prisoners, and killed so many men that the blood splashed all over the clouds and made them as red as a sunset. Quite a lot of it dripped right down on to the earth, and made me wonder if something of the sort had happened before, which would account for that extraordinary statement in Homer that Zeus rained down tears of blood at the thought of Sarpedon's death.

In the end we got tired of chasing them, so we stopped and erected two trophies, one in the middle of the cobweb to commemorate the prowess of the infantry, and one in the clouds to mark the success of our airborne forces. Just as we were doing so, a report came through that Phaethon's unpunctual allies, the cloud-centaurs, were rapidly approaching. When they finally appeared they were a most astonishing sight, for they were a cross between winged horses and human beings. The human part was about as big as the Colossus at Rhodes, and the horse part was roughly the size of a large merchant ship. I had better not tell you how many there were of them, for you would never believe me if I did, but you may as well know that they were led by Sagittarius, the archer in the Zodiac.

Hearing that their allies had been defeated, they sent a message to Phaethon telling him to rally his forces and make a counter-attack. In the mean time, they set the example by promptly spreading out in line and charging the Moon-people before they had time to organize themselves – for they had broken ranks as soon as the rout began, and now they were scattered about all over the place in search of loot. The result was that our entire army was put to flight, the King himself was chased all the way back to his capital and most of his birds lost their lives.

The cloud-centaurs pulled down the trophies and devastated the whole cobweb, capturing me and two of my friends in the process. By this time, Phaethon had returned to the scene of action and erected some trophies of his own, after which we were carried off to the Sun as prisoners of war, our hands securely lashed behind our backs with pieces of cobweb.

The victors decided not to besiege Endymion's capital, but merely to cut off his light supply by building a wall in the middle of the air. The wall in question was composed of a double thickness of cloud, and was so effective that the Moon was totally eclipsed and condemned to a permanent state of darkness. Eventually Endymion was reduced to a policy of appeasement, and sent a message to Phaethon, humbly begging him to take down the wall and not make them spend the rest of their lives in the dark, volunteering to pay a war indemnity and conclude a pact of non-aggression with the Sun, and offering hostages as a guarantee of his good faith.

Phaethon's Parliament met twice to consider these proposals. At the first meeting they passed a resolution rejecting them out of hand; at the second they reversed this decision and agreed to make peace on terms which were ultimately incorporated in the following document:

AN AGREEMENT made this day between the Sun-people and their allies (hereinafter called "The Victors") of the one part and the Moon-people and their allies (hereinafter called "The Vanquished") of the other part

1. The Victors agree to demolish the wall, to refrain in future from invading the Moon and to return their prisoners of war at a fixed charge per head.

2. The Vanquished agree not to violate the sovereign rights of other stars, and not to make war in future upon The Victors, but to assist them in case of attack by a third party, and such assistance is to be reciprocal.

3. The Vanquished undertake to pay to The Victors annually in advance ten thousand bottles of dew, and to commit ten thousand hostages to their keeping.

4. The colony on Lucifer shall be established jointly by both parties, other stars being free to participate if they so wish.

5. The terms of this agreement shall be inscribed on a column of amber, to be erected in the middle of the air on the frontier between the two kingdoms.

SIGNED for and on behalf of the Sun-people
      and their allies
           Rufus T. Fireman
      for and on behalf of the Moon-people
      and their allies
           P.M. Loony

As soon as peace was declared, the wall was taken down and we three prisoners were released. When we got back to the Moon, we were greeted with tears of joy not only by the rest of our party but even by Endymion himself. He was very anxious for me to stay and help him with the colony, and actually offered to let me marry his son – for there are no such things as women on the Moon – but I was intent on getting down to the sea again, and as soon as he realized that I had made up my mind, he gave up trying to keep me. So off we went, after a farewell dinner which lasted for a week.

At this point, I should like to tell you some of the odd things I noticed during my stay on the Moon. First of all, their methods of reproduction: as they have never even heard of women up there, the men just marry other men, and these other men have the babies. The system is that up to the age of twenty-five one acts as a wife, and from then on as a husband.

When a man is pregnant, he carries the child not in his stomach but in the calf of his leg, which grows extremely fat on these occasions. In due course they do a caesarean, and the baby is taken out dead, but it is then brought to life by being placed in a high wind with its mouth wide open. Incidentally, it seems to me that these curious facts of lunar physiology may throw some light on a problem of etymology, for have we not here the missing link between the two apparently unconnected senses of the word calf?

Even more surprising is the method of propagating what are known as Tree-men. This is how it is done: you cut off the father's right testicle and plant it in the ground, where it grows into a large fleshy tree rather like a phallus, except that it has leaves and branches and bears fruit in the form of acorns, which are about eighteen inches long. When the fruit is ripe, it is picked and the babies inside are hatched out.

It is not uncommon up there to have artificial private parts, which apparently work quite well. If you are rich, you have them made of ivory, but the poorer classes have to rub along with wooden ones.

When Moon-people grow old, they do not die. They just vanish into thin air, like smoke – and talking of smoke, I must tell you about their diet, which is precisely the same for everyone. When they feel hungry, they light a fire and roast some frogs on it – for there are lots of these creatures flying about in the air. Then, while the frogs are roasting, they draw up chairs round the fire, as if it were a sort of dining-room table, and gobble up the smoke.

That is all they ever eat, and to quench their thirst they just squeeze some air into a glass and drink that: the liquid produced is rather like dew. They never make water in the other sense, nor do they ever evacuate their bowels, having no hole in that part of their anatomy; and if this makes you wonder what they do with their wives, the answer is that they have a hole in the crook of the knee, conveniently situated immediately above the calf.

Bald men are considered very handsome on the Moon, and long hair is thought absolutely revolting; but on young stars, like the comets, which have not yet lost their hair, it is just the other way round – or so at least I was told by a Comet-dweller who was having a holiday on the Moon when I was there.

I forgot to mention that they wear their beards a little above the knee, and they have not any toenails, for the very good reason that they have not any toes. What they have got, however, is a large cabbage growing just above the buttocks like a tail. It is always in flower, and never gets broken, even if they fall flat on their backs.

When they blow their noses, what comes out is extremely sour honey, and when they have been working hard or taking strenuous exercise, they sweat milk at every pore. Occasionally they turn it into cheese by adding a few drops of the honey.

They also make olive oil out of onions, and the resulting fluid is extremely rich and has a very delicate perfume.

They have any number of vines, which produce not wine but water, for the grapes are made of ice; and there, in my view, you have the scientific explanation of hailstorms, which occur whenever the wind is strong enough to blow the fruit off those vines.

They use their stomachs as handbags for carrying things around in, for they can open and shut them at will. If you look inside one, there is nothing to be seen in the way of digestive organs, but the whole interior is lined with fur so that it can also be used as a centrally heated pram for babies in cold weather.

The upper classes wear clothes made of flexible glass, but this material is rather expensive, so most people have to be content with copper textiles – for there is any amount of copper in the soil, which becomes as soft as wool when soaked in water.

I hardly like to tell you about their eyes, for fear you should think I am exaggerating, because it really does sound almost incredible. Still, I might as well risk it, so here goes: their eyes are detachable, so that you can take them out when you do not want to see anything and put them back when you do. Needless to say, it is not unusual to find someone who has mislaid his own eyes altogether and is always having to borrow someone else's; and those who can afford it keep quite a number of spare pairs by them, just in case. As for ears, the tree-men have wooden ones of their own, and everyone else has to be satisfied with a couple of plane tree leaves instead.

I must just mention one other thing that I saw in the King's palace. It was a large mirror suspended over a fairly shallow tank. If you got into the tank, you could hear everything that was being said on the Earth, and if you looked in the mirror, you could see what was going on anywhere in the world, as clearly as if you were actually there yourself. I had a look at all the people I knew at home, but whether they saw me or not, I really cannot say.

Well, that is what it was like on the Moon. If you do not believe me, go and see for yourself.

Finally we said goodbye to the King and his courtiers, boarded our ship and set sail. As a parting gift, Endymion presented me with two glass shirts, five copper ones and a complete suit of lupin armour, but unfortunately they got lost later on. We were also given air protection by a thousand vulture riders, who escorted us for the first fifty miles of our journey.

After sailing past several islands without stopping, we eventually arrived at Lucifer, where we found an advance party of colonists already in occupation, so we landed there to replenish our water supply. Then we re-embarked and set a course for the Zodiac. This brought us within a few hundred yards of the Sun, and we very much wanted to land there too, but the wind made it impossible. Still, we saw enough to tell us that it was an extremely fertile country, with plenty of rivers and other natural advantages.

While we were coasting along, we were spotted by some cloud-centaurs in Phaethon's employment, who dived down and started circling the ship, but when they heard that we were under the protection of an allied power, they went away again. Our escort of vulture riders had, of course, left us already.

We continued on the same course, but losing height all the time for the next twenty-four hours, and the following evening arrived at a place called Lampborough, which is situated halfway between the Hyades and the Pleiades, and considerably below the Zodiac.

We went ashore, expecting to meet some human beings, but all we saw was a lot of lamps walking about. There were lamps transacting business in the marketplace, and lamps working on the ships in the harbour. Most of them were wretched little creatures, who were obviously pretty dim, but there were one or two of immense power and brilliance, who were clearly the leading lights of the community. Each lamp had its own private house with its name on the door, and we could hear them chatting away to their neighbours over the garden fence. They were all perfectly friendly, and we had several offers of hospitality, but none of us quite liked the idea of eating or sleeping with them.

In the middle of the town was a law court, in which the chief magistrate was holding an all-night session. Various lamps were summoned to appear before him, and those who failed to show up were sentenced to death as deserters: death, of course, meant being blown out. We went in and watched the proceedings for a while, and heard several lamps make excuses for not starting work promptly at lighting-up time. Among those present I suddenly recognized a lamp of my own, so I asked him how things were going at home, and he told me all the latest news.

After spending the night there, we started off again and soon found ourselves among the clouds, where, rather to our surprise, we sighted the famous city of Cloudcuckoobury. The wind was too strong for us to land there, but we gathered that they had just been holding an election for president, and that the successful candidate was a man called Crow.

"So Aristophanes was telling the truth after all," I said to myself. "How wrong I was to doubt him!"

Three days later the sea became clearly visible, but there was still no sign of land, except for a few islands in the air, which were much too hot and bright for us to approach. Finally, about noon on the fourth day, the wind gradually subsided and enabled us to make a perfect landing on the surface of the sea.

It was wonderful to be able to dabble our fingers in the water again, and we immediately celebrated the occasion with what was left of our wine. Then we dived overboard and had a glorious swim, for the sea was quite calm and there were no big waves.

But as so often happens, this apparent change for the better was only the prelude to something infinitely worse. The fine weather continued for another two days, but at dawn on the third we suddenly saw a school of whales approaching from the east. The largest was about a hundred and seventy miles long, and he started coming towards us with his mouth open, churning up the water for miles around into a great cloud of foam, and baring his teeth, which were considerably taller than the biggest phallus you ever saw in your life, as sharp as needles and as white as ivory. We kissed one another goodbye and waited for the inevitable.

The next moment he had gobbled us up, ship and all, but he never got a chance of chewing us, for the ship slipped through one of the gaps between his teeth and sailed straight into his stomach.

At first it was so dark inside that we could not see a thing, but after a while he opened his mouth again and we saw that we were in a sort of cave, which stretched away to an immense distance in every direction and would have been quite capable of accommodating a town with a population of anything up to ten thousand. It was littered with piles of fish and other sea creatures, all mashed up together with sails and anchors and human bones and the remains of ships' cargoes, and in the middle of it was a tract of land which rose into a range of low hills. I suppose it was the sediment of all the muddy water that the whale had swallowed over the years. By this time it was covered with trees, and lots of other plants and vegetables were growing on it. In fact, the whole area, which was about twenty-seven miles in circumference, appeared to be under intensive cultivation. It was alive with various types of seabird, and kingfishers and seagulls were to be seen nesting in the trees.

For a long time we felt far too depressed to do anything, but eventually we pulled ourselves together and put props under the ship, after which we rubbed some sticks together to make a fire, and had as good a meal as we could manage in the circumstances. At least there was no shortage of fish, and we still had some of the water that we had taken on board at Lucifer.

Next morning, we spent the first few hours admiring the view through the monster's mouth, whenever he happened to open it. One moment we would catch sight of some land, the next of some mountains. Sometimes there would be nothing to see but sky, sometimes we would have a glimpse of some islands – from all which we concluded that the whale was dashing about at high speed from one end of the sea to the other. Before long we began to get used to it, and thinking we might as well see all there was to be seen of our new home, I set off with seven others for a stroll through the woods.

We had scarcely gone half a mile before we came across a temple, with an inscription saying that it was dedicated to Poseidon. A little farther on we saw some graves, complete with tombstones, and not far off a spring of fresh water. The next moment we heard a dog barking and noticed some smoke rising above the trees. Assuming that it came from a house of some kind, we began to walk faster and suddenly came face to face with an old man and a boy, who were busily engaged in weeding and watering a kitchen garden.

We came to an abrupt standstill, hardly knowing whether to feel pleased or frightened, and their reaction was evidently much the same, for at first they just stared at us without saying a word. The old man was the first to recover.

"My dear sirs!" he exclaimed. "Who on earth are you? Are you sea gods of some kind, or merely unfortunate human beings like us? Oh yes, that's what we are. We were born and bred on dry land like anyone else, but now we seem to have turned into some species of fish, for here we are swimming about inside this great sea creature! To tell you the truth, I really don't know what's happened to us. I shouldn't be at all surprised to hear that we were dead – but I prefer to think we're still alive."

"We're human beings too, sir, I assure you," I replied. "We haven't been here very long, though – we were only swallowed yesterday – and we were just taking a walk through the woods to see what they were like. However, some good angel seems to have brought us together, so now we've the comfort of knowing we're not the only ones in this situation. But do tell us who you are and how you got here."

"Let's keep all that," he said, "until after dinner."

With these words, he took us into his house, which was quite a comfortable one, with built-in bunks and all the usual conveniences, and gave us an excellent meal of fish, vegetables and fruit. When we had had as much as we wanted, he asked us how we came to be there, so I described the whole series of our adventures, from the beginning of the great storm right up to our arrival in the whale.

"What an amazing story!" he exclaimed when I had finished. "And now I suppose it's my turn. Well, I'm a Cypriot by birth, and one day, many years ago, I started off on a trading expedition to Italy, taking my son here and quite a lot of my servants with me. I had a varied assortment of goods on board a large vessel – you probably noticed the remains of it in the throat as you came in.

"All went well until we were approaching Sicily, but then we were caught in a gale and three days later found ourselves in the Atlantic. There we met the whale, who swallowed our ship with every man on board, and we two were the only survivors. So we buried all the others, built a temple to Poseidon and have been here ever since, spending most of our time growing vegetables to eat, and supplementing our diet with fish and fruit.

"On the whole, the conditions aren't too bad. You can see for yourselves, there's no shortage of timber, and there are several vines in the forest, which make quite decent wine. There are plenty of soft leaves to stuff our pillows and mattresses with, and any amount of firewood.

"When we get bored, we amuse ourselves by laying snares for the birds that fly in through the mouth, or climbing out on to the gills and catching some fresh fish – or merely having a shower-bath, for it's an excellent place for that too. Oh yes, and there's a saltwater lake not far from here, about two miles round and full of all sorts of fish. We often go swimming and sailing there – for we've got a small boat, which I built myself.

"It must be twenty-seven years since we were swallowed, so by now we've got quite used to it. The only trouble is, we simply can't stand the neighbours. They're such an uncivilized lot, one really can't have anything to do with them."

"Do you mean to say," I asked, "that there are some other people living inside this creature?"

"Of course there are," he replied. "Hundreds of them – and an uglier pack of brutes you never saw. The western, that's to say the tail end, part of the forest is inhabited by people who look like kippers, except that they have eyes like eels and faces like lobsters. They live on raw meat and are very aggressive. Over towards the right wall of the stomach is a colony of mermen – I don't know what else to call them, for above the waist they're ordinary human beings, and below it they're just plain lizards. Still, they're much less troublesome than some of the others. On the left are some people with claws instead of hands, and some friends of theirs who have heads like tuna fish. The area in the middle is occupied by crab-like creatures with feet like turbots, who can run very fast and are extremely quarrelsome. Most of the land towards the east, that is, towards the mouth, is uninhabited, as it's liable to be flooded by the sea, but even so those wretched turbot feet have the impudence to charge me five hundred oysters per annum for the lease of it. Well, that's what the neighbours are like, and the problem is, how can one maintain a reasonable standard of life in such conditions?"

"How many of them are there altogether?" I asked.

"Oh, a thousand at the very least," he answered.

"What sort of weapons have they got?"

"None whatever, unless you count fish bones."

"In that case," said I, "our wisest plan would be to go to war with them, for we've got all the latest equipment, and if we can once show them who's master, we'll have no more trouble."

Everyone agreed to this proposal, so we returned to our ship and began to prepare for war. As a quarter day was approaching, we thought the best way of provoking hostilities would be to refuse to pay the rent. Accordingly, when an official arrived to collect it, we merely sent him away with a flea in his ear. This made the crab-men very angry with Scintharus – for that was our host's name – and they came rushing towards us in full force, howling for vengeance. As soon as we realized that they were on the warpath, we armed ourselves and awaited their attack, having previously arranged an ambush of twenty-five men, who had instructions to fall upon the enemy's rear the moment they had gone past.

Everything went according to plan. Our ambushed troops closed in on the crab-men from behind and started cutting them to pieces, while the other twenty-five of us – for Scintharus and his son were taking the places of our two cross-fertilisers – made a savage onslaught from the opposite direction. Eventually we managed to rout them, and chased them all the way back to their holes, killing a hundred and seventy in the process. Our only casualty was the steersman, who was run through from behind with the rib of a red mullet.

That night we camped out on the battlefield, and stuck up a dolphin's vertebral column by way of a trophy. Next morning the news got round to all the other inhabitants of the whale, who joined forces and renewed the attack. On the right wing were the people who looked like kippers, under the command of Field Marshal Anchovy, on the left the people with heads like tuna fish and in the centre the people with claws instead of hands. The mermen had stayed at home, having decided to remain neutral.

We made contact with the enemy not far from the temple of Poseidon, and immediately came to grips with them, uttering blood-curdling yells that went echoing round and round the whale's cavernous interior. It did not take us long to rout our unarmed opponents and chase them back into the forest, and from then on the whole country was under our control. After a while they sent envoys to arrange for the burial of their dead and discuss terms of peace, but we had no intention of making peace just yet, and next day we systematically destroyed every single one of them except the mermen, who scuttled away through the gills and dived into the sea the moment they saw what was going on.

After that we proceeded to explore the country at our leisure, and now that all hostile elements had been eliminated, we settled down to a life of luxury, in which we spent most of our time playing games, or hunting, or cultivating the vines, or picking fruit off the trees. In fact, we were like prisoners in a very comfortable jail, where the regulations allowed one to do exactly what one liked, except escape.

This went on for a year and eight months, but on the fifth day of the ninth month, at the second opening of the whale's mouth – for he opened his mouth regularly once an hour, which was our only method of telling the time – at two o'mouth precisely, as I said, we suddenly heard a tremendous row going on outside, in which we could distinguish shouts of command and the splashing of oars. We were so intrigued that we clambered right up into the mouth and stood immediately behind the teeth, where we had an excellent view of the most amazing spectacle that I have ever seen: giants three hundred feet high sailing about on islands, just as we do on ships.

I know you will think this part of my story quite incredible, but I am going to tell you about it all the same. The islands in question were extremely long, though not particularly high. Each was approximately eleven miles in circumference, and carried a crew of about a hundred and twenty. Some of these were sitting on either side of the island and rowing in perfect time, not with oars, but with enormous cypress trees, complete with all their original branches and leaves. Behind them, at what you might call the stern, was a steersman standing on the top of a hill and operating a bronze rudder about half a mile long, and at the prow were another forty giants or so, fully armed and exactly like human beings, except that they had flames instead of hair, which enabled them to dispense with helmets.

Each island had a lot of trees growing on it, which bellied out in the wind and enabled the helmsman to move his craft in any direction he chose, but the principal motive power was provided by the rowers, who were kept in time by a man specially detailed for the purpose, and could send their island zooming along at a fantastic rate of knots.

At first there were only two or three of these islands to be seen, but eventually about six hundred made their appearance, and as soon as they had taken up their battle stations a great naval action began. Some of them collided head-on, others were rammed amidships and started to sink, and several pairs became inextricably entangled, whereupon the troops posted at the prows boarded one another's islands, and desperate hand-to-hand fighting ensued, in which no prisoners were taken.

Instead of grappling irons they used giant octopuses with cables attached to them, which wound their tentacles round the trees of the enemy island and thus prevented it from getting away. They also bombarded one another with oysters the size of farm carts and sponges a hundred feet in diameter.

Apparently the whole thing had started because Seabooze, the commander of one fleet, had misappropriated a herd of dolphins belonging to Quickswim, the commander of the other, for we could hear them hurling abuse at one another, and each side was using its leader's name as a sort of battle cry. Eventually Quickswim won, after sinking a hundred and fifty enemy islands and capturing another three, complete with their crews. The rest went full speed astern and lit out for the horizon. Their enemies pursued them for a while, but when it began to get dark they gave it up and came back to deal with the wrecks. After taking control of most of the enemy ones, they proceeded to salvage eighty or so of their own which had been sunk, and finally, to commemorate their victory, they stuck up one of the captured islands on top of the whale's head.

That night they camped out on the creature's back, having moored some of their islands to it with cables and left the rest to ride at anchor nearby. Oh yes, they had anchors too – very strong ones, made entirely of glass. Next morning they held a thanksgiving service, dug graves in the whale's skin and buried their dead in them, and eventually sailed away in excellent spirits, singing some sort of triumphal chant.

So much for the battle of the islands.

BOOK II

A FTER A WHILE I GOT rather bored with life inside the whale, and started trying to think of some method of escape. Our first plan was to dig our way out through the creature's right side, but when we had constructed a tunnel nearly half a mile long without getting anywhere, we abandoned that idea and decided instead to set fire to the forest, in the hope that this would kill the whale and thus facilitate our exit. So, working gradually from the tail end towards the mouth, we began committing systematic arson.

For seven days and nights the monster remained completely unaware of it, but after eight or nine days we gathered that he was feeling rather off colour, because he did not open his mouth quite so much. By the tenth day some of the flesh had gone gangrenous and began to stink, and on the twelfth we suddenly realized to our horror that if we did not jam something between his jaws next time he opened his mouth, we ran a serious risk of being buried alive in a corpse.

So before it was too late, we managed to wedge his mouth open with two great wooden beams, after which we proceeded to recommission our ship, stocking up with as much water and other necessaries as possible and inviting Scintharus to take over the job of steersman.

By next morning, the whale was thoroughly dead. We hauled the ship up into the mouth, pushed it through one of the gaps between the teeth, and steadying it with ropes belayed round the teeth themselves, lowered it gently into the sea. Then we climbed on to the creature's back, where, beside the trophy commemorating the sea fight, we made a thank-offering to Poseidon. As there was no wind, we camped out there for the next three days, but on the fourth we returned to our ship and sailed away. During the first few hours, we came across several corpses left over from the battle of the islands, and actually beached our ship on one of them, in order to take its measurements – which surprised us considerably.

When we had been sailing along for several days with a gentle breeze behind us, a bitter wind sprang up from the north and caused such a sharp drop in temperature that the whole sea froze solid – not merely on the surface, but to a depth of approximately four hundred fathoms, so that one could safely step out of the ship and walk about on the ice.

The wind went on blowing steadily, and we were beginning to find the cold quite unbearable, when Scintharus suddenly had a bright idea. On his advice, we dug a huge cave under the water, in which we lit a fire and lived very comfortably for the next four weeks or so on a diet of fish, which we hacked out of the sea around us. When supplies finally ran out, we emerged from our shelter, prised the ship out of the ice, put on full sail and went skidding along over the slippery surface as smoothly and pleasantly as if we had been sailing in the conventional manner.

Five days later there was a thaw, and the sea turned back into water. We continued our voyage, and about thirty-four miles farther on came to a small desert island, where we collected some fresh water – for we had used up the last lot – and shot a couple of wild bulls before putting to sea again. The bulls in question wore their horns immediately below their eyes, in accordance with Momus's recommendation, instead of on top of their heads.

Shortly afterwards, we entered a sea of milk, in which we sighted a white island with large numbers of vines growing on it. This island turned out to be an enormous hunk of cheese, of rather tough consistency (as we soon found out when we started eating it) and measuring nearly three miles in circumference. There were plenty of grapes on the vines, but when we tried squeezing them in the hope of making some wine, all that came out was milk.

In the middle of the island someone had built a temple. The inscription informed us that it was dedicated to Galatea, the lady whose complexion has been described as whiter than cream cheese. We stayed there for five days, living quite literally on the fat of the land and drinking milk from the grapes, and learnt that the whole place belonged to the sea nymph Gorgonzola. Apparently Poseidon gave it to her after their divorce, by way of alimony.

On the morning of the sixth day we started off again, and for the next two days were wafted by a gentle breeze over an almost waveless sea. Then, just as we had noticed that we were no longer sailing through milk, but through salt water of the normal colour, we saw a lot of people running towards us. They were exactly like us except that their feet were made of cork – and that, I suspect, was the reason why they were called Corkfeet. We were most surprised at first to see them bounding along over the waves instead of sinking through them, but they seemed to take it absolutely for granted. They came up and spoke to us in our own language, explaining that they lived in the Isle of Cork and were in a great hurry to get back there. They trotted along beside us for a while, then, wishing us bon voyage, turned off to the left and were soon out of sight.

A few hours later some islands came into view. Quite near us on the left was a town built on top of a huge round cork, which we took to be the place that our fellow travellers had been making for. Farther away towards the right were five great mountainous islands which looked as if they were on fire, and straight ahead of us, but at least fifty miles away, a long low island appeared on the horizon.

When we got a bit closer to it, we became aware of a wonderful perfume floating about in the atmosphere, of much the same kind, no doubt, as the one that Herodotus describes as emanating from Arabia. To give you some idea how pleasant it was, it was like smelling roses, narcissi, hyacinths, lilies, violets, myrtles, bays and flowers of the wild vine all at the same time. It made us feel that our luck had turned at last, and following our delighted noses, we drew gradually nearer and nearer to the island.

Soon we were close enough to make out several large harbours, in which the water was absolutely calm, and several limpid streams flowing gently into the sea. Then we saw meadows and woods, and heard birds singing on the shore and on the branches of the trees. The whole atmosphere of the place was light and airy, owing to a pleasant breeze which kept the trees in perpetual motion and blew through the branches with a delightful humming sound, rather like the effect of hanging up a flute in the open air. And far away in the distance we could hear a confused uproar which was not in the least alarming, for it was only the sort of noise you get at a party when some of the guests are playing flutes or guitars, and some of them are singing, and the rest are just clapping their hands in time with the music.

We found it all so attractive that we did not hesitate to drop anchor in one of the harbours and go ashore, leaving

Scintharus and two others on board to look after the ship. As we were walking across a flowery meadow, we were stopped and arrested by the local police, who handcuffed us with daisy chains – which are the most powerful form of constraint employed in those parts – and took us off for trial before the chief magistrate. On the way there, they informed us that we were on the Island of the Blessed, and that the magistrate's name was Rhadamanthus.

When we arrived at the court, we found that there were three other cases to be heard before ours came up. The point at issue in the first was whether Ajax Major should be allowed to mix with the other heroes or not, in view of the fact that he had gone mad and committed suicide. After hearing all the arguments for and against, Rhadamanthus finally decided that the accused should be given a dose of hellebore and remanded for psychological treatment by Hippocrates until such time as he should recover his sanity, when he should be free to join the other heroes.

The second was a matrimonial case, in which both Theseus and Menelaus claimed conjugal rights over Helen. The verdict was that she should cohabit with Menelaus, on the ground that he had suffered considerable inconvenience and danger on her account, and also that Theseus had three wives already, namely Hippolyta, Phaedra and Ariadne.

The third case was a question of precedence between Alexander the Great and Hannibal. Rhadamanthus gave his verdict in favour of Alexander, who was then allotted a throne beside Cyrus I of Persia.

At last it was our turn, and Rhadamanthus asked us what excuse we could give for daring to set foot in that holy place while we were still alive, so we told him the whole story. He adjourned the case for several hours while he consulted with his colleagues on the bench, who included, among others, Aristides the Just. Having finally made up his mind, he delivered his verdict as follows:

"For your folly in leaving home and for your idle curiosity, you will be called to account when you die. In the mean time, you may remain here and share the privileges of the heroes for a period not exceeding seven months."

As he spoke these words, our handcuffs fell off of their own accord. We were then formally set at liberty, and escorted into the town to join the heroes.

The town in question is built entirely of gold, except for the outer wall, which is of emerald and contains seven gates, each composed of a solid chunk of cinnamon. The whole area inside the wall is paved with ivory, all the temples are of beryl, and the altars, on which they usually sacrifice a hundred oxen at a time, consist of single slabs of amethyst. The town is encircled by a river of best-quality perfume, nearly two hundred feet across and approximately ninety feet deep, so that you can swim about in it without any risk of stubbing your toe on the bottom. By way of baths, they have large glass houses heated by burning cinnamon, with hot and cold dew laid on.

Their clothes are made of very fine cobwebs, dyed crimson, but they have not any bodies to put them on, for the town is exclusively inhabited by disembodied spirits. However, insubstantial as they are, they give an impression of complete solidity, and move and think and speak like ordinary human beings. Altogether, it is as if their naked souls were walking about clothed in the outward semblance of their bodies, for until you try touching them, it is quite impossible to detect their incorporeal nature. I suppose the best way of putting it would be to say that they are like walking shadows – except, of course, that they are not black.

Nobody grows old there, for they all stay the age they were when they first arrived, and it never gets dark. On the other hand, it never gets really light either, and they live in a sort of perpetual twilight, such as we have just before sunrise. Instead of four seasons, they have only one: for with them it is always spring, and the only wind that blows comes from the west. All kinds of flowers grow there, and all kinds of garden trees, especially shady ones. The vines bear fruit twelve times a year – in other words, once a month – and we were given to understand that the pomegranate trees, the apple trees and all the other fruit trees bore fruit no fewer than thirteen times a year, for two separate crops were normally produced in the month of Minober. As for the corn, instead of ordinary ears it sprouts mushroom-shaped loaves of bread, all ready to eat.

Scattered about the town are three hundred and sixty-five water springs, an equal number of honey springs, five hundred scent springs (but these, I admit, are rather smaller than the others), seven rivers of milk and eight rivers of wine. In spite of these urban amenities, however, most of the social life goes on outside the town, in a place called the Elysian Fields, which is a meadow beautifully situated in the middle of a wood. Under the shade of this wood, which is full of all sorts of different trees, a delightful party is permanently in progress.

The guests recline at their ease on beds of flowers, and are waited on by the winds, which do everything but serve the wine. However, there is no difficulty about that, for there are plenty of big glass trees all round. In case you do not know what glass trees are, they are trees made of very clear glass, which bear fruit in the form of wineglasses of every conceivable shape and size. So every guest picks one or two of these glasses the moment he arrives, and puts them down beside him, whereupon they immediately become full of wine. That takes care of the drink problem, and the floral decorations are arranged by the nightingales and other songbirds from the neighbouring meadows, which pick up flowers in their beaks and rain them down over the guests, singing sweetly all the while.

Finally, the heroes are even saved the trouble of putting on their own scent by the following ingenious system: specially absorbent clouds suck up perfume from the five hundred springs and from the river, after which they go and hover over the party; then the winds give them a gentle squeeze, and down comes the scent in a fine spray like dew.

After dinner, they usually have some kind of musical or literary performance, and their favourite turn is Homer reciting his own poems – for he is generally to be found there, sitting next to Odysseus. They also have choral singing by young boys and girls, conducted and accompanied by someone like Eunomus, or Arion, or Anacreon, or Stesichorus, who has, I am happy to say, been forgiven by Helen for the rude things he wrote about her. When the boys and girls have done their stuff, the floor is taken by a choir of swans and swallows and nightingales, who sing to what you might call a woodwind accompaniment, that is, to the music of the wind blowing through the branches of the trees.

But what really makes the party go with a swing is the fact that there are two springs in that meadow, one of laughter and the other of pleasure. So the first thing a guest does when he gets there is to take a sip from each of these springs, and from then on he never stops laughing and having a wonderful time.

And now I want to tell you about some of the distinguished people I saw there. Among those present were all the demigods, and all the Greek kings who took part in the Trojan War, except for Ajax Minor, who was said to be on one of the Islands of the Damned, serving a sentence for rape. There were also several foreigners, including both the Cyruses from Persia, Anacharsis from Scythia, Zamolxis from Thrace and Pompilius Numa from Italy. Then there was Lycurgus from Sparta, and all the Seven Sages except Periander.

I noticed Socrates having a chat with Nestor and Palamedes. He was surrounded by a group of extremely attractive young men, among whom I recognized Hyacinthus, Narcissus and Hylas. I got the impression that he was in love with Hyacinthus, for he was always firing difficult questions at him; but whatever the motive for them, these discussion classes of his had apparently made him most unpopular with Rhadamanthus, who had often threatened to banish him from the island if he did not stop talking shop and ruining the atmosphere of the party with his peculiar brand of irony.

There was no sign of Plato, and I was told later that he had gone to live in his *Republic*, where he was cheerfully submitting to his own *Laws*. But hedonists like Aristippus and Epicurus were naturally the life and soul of the party: they were such absolutely charming fellows, and so easy to get along with. Aesop was much in demand for his talents as a raconteur, and Diogenes had so far modified his views that he had married Lais, the courtesan, and was always getting drunk and trying to dance on the table.

None of the Stoics were present. Rumour had it that they were still clambering up the steep hill of virtue, and I heard that Chrysippus would in any case not be allowed on the island until he had taken at least four doses of hellebore.

As for the Sceptics, it appeared that they were extremely anxious to get there, but still could not quite make up their minds whether or not the island really existed. I suspect that they were also rather afraid of what Rhadamanthus might do to them, for having talked so much about "suspension of judgement", they probably feared that he might turn out to be a hanging judge. In spite of this, several of them had apparently started out in company with people who had in fact arrived, but either they had been too lazy to keep up with the others and so got left behind, or else they had changed their minds and turned back when they were halfway there.

Well, I think that covers all the most interesting people that I met there, and it only remains to say that the most respected member of the community was Achilles, with Theseus a close runner-up.

And now perhaps you would like to hear something about their attitude to sex. They see nothing indecent in sexual intercourse, whether heterosexual or homosexual, and indulge in it quite openly, in full view of everyone. The only exception was Socrates, who was always swearing that his relations with young men were purely platonic, but nobody believed him for a moment, and Hyacinthus and Narcissus gave first-hand evidence to the contrary. As for the women, they are shared indiscriminately by all the men, and there are no such things as jealous husbands. In that respect, at least, they are all good Communists. Similarly, the boys co-operate freely with anyone who makes advances to them, and never raise the slightest objection.

I had not been there for more than two or three days before I seized an opportunity of going up to Homer and asking him, among other things, what country he really came from, explaining that this was still a great subject of literary research.

"Don't I know it!" he said. "One school of thought claims that I come from Chios, another from Smyrna and a third from Colophon. In point of fact, I come from Babylon, and my real name is Tigranes, which means 'pigeon' in Babylonian. My present nickname dates from an occasion when I was carried off to Greece as a hostage. Within a few days I'd managed to escape and find my way home again, and after that my friends never called me anything but Homer."

I then asked if the textural experts were right in rejecting certain lines in his poems as spurious.

"Of course not," he replied. "I wrote every word of them. The trouble about these wretched editors is that they've got no taste."

Having satisfied my curiosity on this point, I asked him what was the precise significance of the use of the word wrath in the opening sentence of the *Iliad*.

"No significance whatsoever," he answered. "It was the first word that came into my head."

After that I wanted to know if the *Odyssey* was, as many critics think, an earlier work than the *Iliad*.

"Certainly not," said Homer.

There was no need to ask if he was really blind, for I could see for myself that he was nothing of the sort, but I questioned him closely about several other things, for whenever he seemed to have a free moment I used to go and talk to him, and he was delightfully frank in all his answers – especially after he won that lawsuit of his. You see, Thersites brought an action against him for making fun of him in the *Iliad*, but the plaintiff rather overstated his case by suing him, not for libel, but for assault and battery, and Odysseus, who appeared as counsel for the defence, had no difficulty in getting his friend off.

About this time, there were two new arrivals. The first was Pythagoras, who after seven transmigrations of soul had finally completed his life cycle. I noticed that the whole of his right side was made of pure gold. His application for membership was accepted, though there was some doubt whether his name should be entered as Pythagoras or Euphorbus, as it originally was. The second was Empedocles, looking rather the worse for wear after being thoroughly cooked in Mount Etna. In spite of all his efforts to gain admission, this application was turned down flat.

Shortly afterwards, the heroes held their annual funeral games to celebrate their own deaths. The programme was arranged by Achilles and Theseus, who had both had a lot of experience in that line. It would take too long to go through all the events, but I will just give you a rapid summary. The wrestling competition was won by Hercules's son Carus, who managed to beat Odysseus in the finals. The boxing was a draw between Arius the Egyptian (the one who is buried at Corinth) and Epeus. No prize was offered for all-in wrestling, and who won the mile I simply cannot remember. As for the poetry competition, Homer's entry was by far the best, but for some reason or other the prize was awarded to Hesiod. Incidentally, all the prizes in question were crowns of peacocks' feathers.

Just as the games were ending, a report came through that the convicts on the Islands of the Damned had overpowered their warders and broken out, and were heading for the Island of the Blessed. The ringleaders were said to be Phalaris, Busiris, Diomedes of Thrace and a lot of other unpleasant characters like Sciron and Sinis, who used to amuse himself by stringing up passers-by on the tops of pine trees.

Rhadamanthus immediately instructed the heroes to fall in on the beach, under the command of Theseus, Achilles and Ajax Major, who had responded satisfactorily to psychological treatment. A battle then took place between the opposing forces, and the heroes won a resounding victory, for which Achilles was largely responsible. Socrates, however, who was stationed on the right wing, also put up a very good show – far better than he did at the Battle of Delium, for instead of running away when he saw the enemy approaching, he stood his ground and looked them firmly in the eye, on the strength of which he was afterwards awarded a garden of honour in the suburbs, where he collected all his friends and held innumerable discussion classes. I believe he called it his Academy for the Corruption of the Dead.

The escaped convicts were rearrested and sent back to serve even heavier sentences, and Homer wrote an epic poem on the subject of the battle. When I finally said goodbye to him, he gave me a copy of it for publication over here, but unfortunately it got lost, like everything else. However, I can still remember the first few lines, which went like this:

Of hell's first revolution, and the fright
Of that rebellious crew, when heroes dead
Repulsed them, and preserved their blissful isle,
Sing, heavenly Muse!

In accordance with local tradition, we celebrated the victory by eating enormous quantities of baked beans – all except Pythagoras, who registered his disapproval of our bean feast by sitting apart and refusing to eat a thing.

When we had been there six months and were halfway through the seventh, another sensational incident took place. Scintharus's son, Cinyras, had by this time grown into a very good-looking young man and developed a violent passion for Helen. She was obviously madly in love with him too, for they were always exchanging meaning glances across the dinner table and drinking each other's health, or getting up and going for walks in the wood by themselves. Eventually Cinyras felt so desperate about it that he made up his mind to run away with her. She was all for it, and their plan was to go and live on one of the neighbouring islands, either the Isle of Cork or the Isle of Cheese. Three of my most enterprising associates were also in on the plot, but Scintharus had not been let into the secret, for his son knew that he would only try to stop him.

So one night, as soon as it got dark – I was in no condition to interfere, for I had fallen asleep over my wine – they slipped away when the others were not looking, took Helen on board our ship and hurriedly put to sea. About midnight, Menelaus woke up and felt for his wife. Finding she had disappeared, he yelled for his brother, and went rushing off with him to tell Rhadamanthus. Just before dawn the coastguards reported that the ship was still in sight, so Rhadamanthus promptly detailed fifty heroes to embark in a fast vessel, constructed of a single stalk of asphodel, and set off in pursuit. The heroes rowed like mad, and about midday overtook the runaway couple just as they were entering the sea of milk – in fact they very nearly got away with it.

Having taken our ship in tow, using a daisy chain as a towrope, the heroes rowed back to the island, where Helen was escorted ashore in floods of tears, feeling terribly embarrassed and covering her face in her hands, while Cinyras and his three accomplices were brought before Rhadamanthus. After satisfying himself that there were no other accessories to the crime, he sentenced them to forty strokes of the mallow, and transportation to the Islands of the Damned. The court also decided to cancel our immigration permit, and give us twenty-four hours' notice to leave the island.

I was so depressed at the thought of leaving all those good things behind me and starting off on my travels again that I burst into tears – until I was informed by the bench that in a very few years I should come back to them, and that a throne and a couch in the Elysian Fields were being reserved for me in advance. This comforted me a little, and after the trial I went up to Rhadamanthus and begged him to let me know what Fate had in store for me, or at least to give me some help with my navigation. He told me that I had a long way to go yet, and a great many dangers to face, but that I should get home eventually, though he would not like to say exactly when.

"You see those islands?" he said, pointing them out to me. "Well, those five with the flames coming out of them are the Islands of the Damned, and that sixth one in the distance is the Island of Dreams. Beyond that again is Ogygia, where Calypso lives, but you can't see it from here. If you carry straight on past all seven of them, you'll come to a great continent on the opposite side of the world from where you live. There you'll have some very odd experiences and meet some very peculiar people, most of them quite uncivilized, and in due course you'll find your way back to Europe."

He then presented me with a mallow which he had pulled up out of the ground, and told me to pray to it in times of danger. He also gave me a lot of good advice on how to behave when I finally got home, such as never to use a sword to poke the fire, never to eat lupins and never to sleep with boys above the age of eighteen.

"Keep those rules in mind," he concluded, "and you can be sure of coming back here."

So I got everything ready for the voyage, and that night the heroes gave us a farewell dinner. Next morning I went up to Homer and asked him to write me a couple of lines suitable for an inscription. He was only too glad to oblige, and I inscribed them on a tablet of beryl, which I put up near the harbour. They read as follows:

Lucian came here, saw all there was to see,
Then sailed back home across the wine-dark sea.

In spite of the court order, we were allowed to spend one more night on the island, but next day we really did have to go, and all the heroes were there to see us off.

Just before I went on board, Odysseus came up to me and, when Penelope was looking the other way, slipped a letter into my hand, addressed:

Calypso,
Island of Ogygia.

Rhadamanthus had thoughtfully sent Nauplius, the famous pilot, with us, in case we landed on one of the Islands of the Damned and the authorities arrested us, under the impression that we were there in a different capacity. The wisdom of this precaution struck us very forcibly when we exchanged the scented atmosphere of the Island of the Blessed for a horrible smell of burning.

It suggested the simultaneous combustion of pitch, sulphur and petroleum, combined with the roasting of human flesh, and we found it almost unbearable. The air was black with smoke, and a fine rain of pitch started coming down all over us. Then we began to hear the crack of whips and the screams of countless souls in torment.

Well, I do not know what the other islands were like, but the one we landed on was surrounded by steep cliffs, all dry and stony, without any sign of trees or water. However, we managed to climb up over the rocks by a path overgrown with thorns and thistles, and picked our way across some incredibly ugly country until we came to the prison itself.

Before going in, we stopped and stared in amazement at its extraordinary topography. The whole area of ground inside it sprouted a thick crop of sharp knives and stakes, and was enclosed by three rivers, the outer one of mud, the middle one of blood and the inner one of fire. This last was so wide as to be quite impassable, flowed exactly like water, and was furrowed with waves like the sea. There were lots of fish swimming about in it, some like big torches, and others like live coals, which were apparently known as coaleys.

The only way in was across a narrow bridge spanning all three rivers, which was guarded by Timon of Athens, but Nauplius boldly led the way past him, and started pointing out some of the prisoners who were receiving punishment. Many of them were kings, but just as many were ordinary people like ourselves, and we actually recognized one or two of them. For instance, we saw Cinyras strung up by his offending part over a smoky fire.

We were then taken on a conducted tour of the whole prison, and given a summary of each prisoner's crimes. It appeared that the worst punishments of all were reserved for those who had written untrue stories, a category which included Ctesias of Cnidos and Herodotus. As my conscience was absolutely clear in that respect, I was able to watch the poor fellows' sufferings without any serious fears for my own future, but it was a horrible sight all the same, so we got away as soon as we could and returned to our ship, after which we said goodbye to Nauplius and set sail for the Island of Dreams.

We soon caught sight of it not far ahead of us, but its outlines remained blurred and shadowy, as though it was still a long way off, and like a dream it kept retreating as we approached, and doing its best to disappear in the distance. Finally, however, we managed to overtake it, and late that afternoon we came to anchor in the Harbour of Sleep and landed near the ivory gates, not far from the temple of the Cock. We set off immediately to explore the town, and saw all sorts of dreams walking about the streets. But before I tell you about them, I want to describe the town itself, since nobody but Homer has ever so much as mentioned its existence, and his account is not entirely accurate.

All round the town is a forest of tree-like poppies and mandragoras with lots of bats nesting in the branches – for no other form of bird-life is to be found on the island. Close under the city walls, which are very high and all the colours of the rainbow, flows the River of Darkness, and beside one of the city gates is a spring called the Fountain of the Log, and another called the Well of the Eight Hours.

Talking of gates, by the way, Homer was quite wrong when he said that there were only two of them. There are in fact four, two opening on to the Plain of Inertia, one of steel and one of earthenware, and two giving access to the harbour and the sea, one of horn and one of ivory. The landward gates are used as exits for nightmares, and the seaward ones for true and false dreams. Needless to say, we went in by the gate of horn, which is exclusively reserved for dreams of the former type.

On the right as you enter the town is the temple of Night, for she and the Cock are the two great local deities, and on your left is the palace of Sleep, who is the real governor of the island, although he delegates some of his authority to a couple of gentlemen called Muddlehead and Show-off. In the centre of the marketplace is a spring called the Fountain of Coma, and just behind it is the temple of Reality and Illusion, where the residents go for analysis by a specially appointed dream-interpreter called Contradiction.

As for the dreams themselves, they varied enormously in character and appearance. Some were tall and handsome, with soft and beautiful complexions, and some were just ugly little toughs. Some seemed to be made of pure gold, and some were obviously cheap and shoddy. One or two of them had wings, and looked genuinely superhuman, while others were merely dressed up to represent kings and gods and so on.

We recognized several of our recurrent dreams, who came up and greeted us like old friends and invited us into their houses. There they put us to sleep and gave us a reception which was royal in every sense of the word, for they promised to make us kings and treated us as if we were kings already. Some of them were even kind enough to take us back to our homes for an hour or two, so that we could see how our families were getting on.

We stayed with them for a month, fast asleep and having a glorious time. Then suddenly there was a great crash of thunder which woke us all up. We jumped out of bed, ran back to our ship, and pausing only to take a fresh stock of food on board, set sail for the island of Ogygia.

We arrived there two days later, but before going ashore I opened the letter that Odysseus had given me and read its contents, which were as follows:

My darling Calypso,
I thought you might like to know what's been happen-
ing to me since I said goodbye to you and sailed away
on that home-made raft of mine. Well, first of all I was
shipwrecked, but a charming young lady called Leucothea
saved my life and helped me to get ashore. I landed in
Phaeacia, and the people there were good enough to
arrange transport back to Ithaca, where I found a lot of
young men living at my expense and making passes at my
wife. I'd just about finished killing them when I was killed
myself by Telegonus, who's apparently a son of mine by
Circe, though I didn't know it at the time. So now I'm on
the Island of the Blessed, wishing to goodness I'd never
left you and kicking myself for turning down your offer
of immortality. But as soon as I get a chance, I'm going
to slip away from here and come and see you.
Yours ever,
Odysseus

There was also a PS suggesting that she might like to give us a meal while we were there.

We started walking inland, and it did not take us long to find her cave, for it was exactly as Homer described it, and there she was in the doorway spinning wool. I handed her the letter, and the first thing she did when she had read it was to burst into tears. But, after a while, she remembered her duties as a hostess and invited us in to dinner. The food was excellent, and while we were eating it she asked us a lot of questions about Odysseus, and also about Penelope – for instance, what did she look like, and was she really as well behaved as Odysseus used to make out? We gave her the sort of answers that we thought she wanted to hear, and then went and spent the night on the beach beside our ship.

Next morning we set sail in a very high wind, and after battling with it for a couple of days, were unlucky enough to run into some pirates. They were savages from one of the neighbouring islands, who evidently made a practice of attacking all the shipping in their area. Their own ships were made of enormous dried pumpkins, about ninety feet in diameter, hollowed out and fitted with bamboo masts and pumpkin leaves for sails.

Two of these vessels came bearing down on us and started bombarding us with pumpkin pips, which wounded many of us severely. However, we managed to give as good as we got, and towards midday we sighted several other vessels coming up behind them, which apparently belonged to some enemies of theirs, for as soon as they saw them they lost all interest in us and prepared to fight them instead. We seized this opportunity to sail away at full speed, leaving them hard at it. It was fairly obvious who was going to win, for the new arrivals outnumbered their opponents by five to two, and their ships were much stronger, consisting as they did of hollowed-out nutshells, which were also about ninety feet in diameter.

As soon as we had got well away from them, we dressed our casualties' wounds, and from then on went fully armed day and night, for we never knew when we might not be attacked. Sure enough, just before sunset twenty more pirates suddenly darted out at us from an apparently unin-habited island. They were mounted on large dolphins, which neighed like horses as they bounded across the waves. The pirates quickly surrounded our ship and started pelting us at close range with dried squids and crabs' eyes, but as soon as we let fly with our arrows and javelins, so many of them were wounded that the whole lot turned tail and fled back to the island.

About midnight, when the sea was very calm, we inadvertently ran aground on a halcyon's nest. It was nearly seven miles in circumference, and the bird that was sitting on it was not much smaller. We interrupted her in the process of incubating her eggs, and she flew up into the air with a melancholy cry, creating such a draught with her wings that she practically sank our ship. As soon as it was light, we disembarked and went for a walk round the nest, which consisted of a vast number of trees plaited together to form a sort of raft. On it were five hundred eggs, each about the size of a barrel, from which impatient chirpings could already be heard. So we broke one open with an axe, and hatched out a chick approximately twenty times as big as a vulture.

A few miles farther on we were startled by some most unusual phenomena. The goose-shaped projection at the stern of the ship suddenly started flapping its wings and quacking. Simultaneously, Scintharus, who had been bald for years, developed a fine head of hair, and most surprising of all, the mast began putting out branches, and some figs and some black grapes appeared at the top of it – though unfortunately they were not quite ripe. Naturally we were rather taken aback, having no idea what disasters these portents were meant to portend, so we just prayed to the gods to avert them, whatever they were.

We sailed another fifty miles and sighted a huge thick forest of pines and cypresses. They were growing, not on dry land, as we thought at first, but in the middle of the bottomless deep – so of course they had no roots. In spite of this disadvantage, they somehow contrived to keep vertical and stay absolutely still: presumably they were floating. When we got nearer and began to realize what we were up against, we felt completely baffled, for the trees grew too close together for us to sail between them, and by that time it seemed equally impossible to turn back.

I climbed to the top of the tallest tree I could find, to see what happened the other side of the forest, and discovered that after about five miles of it there was open sea again. In the circumstances, we decided that our only hope was to get the ship up on top of the trees, where the foliage looked quite thick enough to support it, and somehow carry it across to the other side. So that is what we did. We tied a good strong rope round the prow, then climbed to the top of the trees, and with some difficulty hauled the ship up after us. Once we had got it there, things were easier then we had expected. All we had to do was spread our sails, and the wind pushed us along across the branches – in fact, it was just like sailing through the water, only of course rather slower. It reminded me of a striking line in a poem by Antimachus:

They voyaged onward o'er a sea of leaves.

Having thus solved the problem of the forest, we lowered our ship into the water again, and continued our journey through a clear and sparkling sea until we came to a deep cleft in the ocean, rather like one of those fissures that sometimes develop on land as a result of earthquakes. We hastily took in sail, but our momentum carried us right up to the edge, and we very nearly went over. Peeping down, we saw to our surprise and horror that there was a sheer drop of approximately 600,000 feet, as if the sea had been sliced in half from top to bottom.

However, when we looked around a bit, we saw, not far off on the right, a sort of bridge of water running across from one side to the other. So we rowed towards it, and with our hearts in our mouths just managed to get over – but we never thought we would make it!

Beyond the chasm the sea looked smooth and inviting, and after a while we sighted a small island which offered good landing facilities and appeared to be inhabited. So we went ashore and started walking inland in search of food and water, as our supplies had run out. Well, we soon found some water, but there was no sign of food, except for a lot of mooing in the distance. Assuming that this indicated a herd of cows somewhere, we advanced in the direction of the sound and suddenly came face to face with a crowd of savages. They were human beings with heads and horns like cattle – in fact, just like the Minotaur.

The moment they saw us, they put down their heads and charged. Three of us were killed, but the rest of us got safely back to the ship. There we collected some weapons – for we had no intention of letting our friends' deaths go unavenged – and then returned to make a counter-attack. This time we managed to catch them off their guard, for they were just preparing to dine on our late companions, so we let out a sudden yell and fell upon them, killing at least fifty and capturing two prisoners of war, whom we took on board our ship.

As we had still failed to find any food, someone suggested that we should make do with the prisoners, but I would not allow it and insisted on keeping them alive, until eventually the enemy sent ambassadors to discuss terms for their repatriation – at least we gathered that this was what they meant, though they could not do anything but point at the prisoners and moo pathetically. So we handed them over in exchange for a lot of cheese, some dried fish, some onions and four three-legged deer. The latter had the usual number of back legs, but only one in front.

We stayed there for the rest of that day, and the following morning put to sea again. Before long there were various indications that we were approaching land – fish swimming closer to the surface, birds flying about and so on. Shortly afterwards, we saw some men practising a most unusual form of navigation, which might be called "paddling your own canoe", except that you are the canoe, and there is no need to paddle. I will tell you how it is done. You float on your back in the water, elevate the appropriate organ – which in their case is surprisingly large – to an angle of ninety degrees, attach a sail to this improvised mast and go scudding along before the wind, holding the sheet in one hand.

Then we saw some other people sitting on corks and being drawn along by dolphins, harnessed together in pairs. They seemed perfectly friendly and not at all nervous, for they drove straight up to us and inspected our ship from every possible angle, having apparently never seen such a thing before.

That evening we landed on another small island, which appeared to be inhabited exclusively by women. They greeted us in our own language, shook us warmly by the hands and kissed us. They were all young and pretty, and most attractively dressed in long flowing garments which reached right down to the ground. They told us that the island was called Noholdsbarred, and the town itself Waterbitch, and each of them asked one of us to spend the night with her.

I could not help feeling that there was something fishy about this arrangement, so before following my hostess indoors I took a quick look round – and came across a large pile of human bones and skulls!

Well, I did not want to raise the alarm just yet, but I got out my mallow and prayed to it earnestly – for if this was not a "time of danger" I did not know what was. A few minutes later, as my hostess was bustling about the kitchen getting dinner ready, I spotted that she had donkey's hooves instead of ordinary feet. I immediately drew my sword, grabbed hold of her and tied her up securely, and then subjected her to a thorough cross-examination. At first she refused to say anything, but in the end she confessed that she belonged to a species of mermaid known as Assfeetida, which lives on a diet of human flesh.

"Our usual system," she added, "is to get our guests drunk, then go to bed with them and kill them while they're asleep."

On the strength of this information, I climbed onto the roof of the house, leaving her still tied up, and shouted for my companions. As soon as they arrived, I explained the situation, directed their attention to the heap of bones and took them indoors to see my prisoner – who promptly turned into water and disappeared. Just to see what would happen, I ran the water through with my sword, and it instantly became blood.

That was enough for us. We raced back to the ship and put to sea, and next morning, just as it was getting light, we sighted what we took to be the mainland. So after kneeling down and saying a prayer, we began to discuss our future policy. Some of us wanted to make a token landing, just so that we could say we had been there, and then go straight home. Another suggestion was that we should abandon the ship and start exploring the interior to see what the natives were like.

While we were arguing about it, we were suddenly overtaken by a violent storm, which dashed our ship against the rocky coast and completely broke it up. All we could do was grab our weapons and anything else that came to hand, and strike out for the shore. Thus we finally landed on the continent at the other side of the world; and what happened to us there, I will tell you in another book.

LUCIUS, OR THE ASS

LUCIUS, OR THE ASS

I ONCE HAD OCCASION TO GO to Thessaly on business in connection with my father's estate. I had a horse to carry me and my luggage, and one servant to look after me. On the way there I got into conversation with a party of Thessalians who were travelling back to a place called Hypata. When we finally came in sight of the town, I asked them if they happened to know a man who lived there called Hipparchus, explaining that I had a letter of introduction to him and hoped he might put me up for the night. They replied that they knew him well and would show me where he lived, but warned me that he was terribly mean, for although he had plenty of money, he kept only one servant and made his wife do most of the work.

Just as we were entering the town, they pointed to quite a decent little house with a garden in front of it.

"That's where he lives," they said. "So long." And off they went.

I walked up the garden path and knocked on the front door. After a long time it was answered by a woman whom I took to be Hipparchus's wife.

"Is Hipparchus at home?" I asked.

"He is," said the woman, "but who are you, and what business is it of yours?"

"I've got a letter for him from Decrianus, Professor of Rhetoric at Patrae."

"Wait here," she snapped, and went back into the house, slamming the door behind her.

After a while, she reappeared and told me to come in. I found Hipparchus sitting on a narrow bench in front of an empty table, for apparently I had interrupted them just as they were about to have dinner. I shook hands with him and gave him the letter.

"So you're one of Decrianus's students, are you?" he said, when he had read it. "A very old friend of mine – one of the best fellows in the whole of Greece. I'm delighted to hear that things are going well with him. Well, Lucius, you can see for yourself that we haven't got a very big house here, but it suits us very well, and if you're prepared to put up with it, I think we can make you reasonably comfortable. Palaestra," he added, turning to the maid, "please take my young friend to his room, and bring in his luggage, if he has any. And don't forget to show him where the bathroom is – for I expect he'd like a wash after his long journey."

Palaestra showed me into a very pleasant little room and pointed to the bed.

"You can sleep there," she said, "and I'll put a campbed beside it for your servant, and fetch an extra pillow."

When she had brought in the luggage, I asked her to give the horse some oats, and went off to have a wash, after which I returned to the living room, where Hipparchus took me by the hand and made me sit down beside him. The food was not at all bad, and the wine was excellent. After dinner we went on talking and drinking, as one usually does on these occasions, until it was time for bed.

Next morning Hipparchus asked me where exactly I was trying to get to – or was I planning to spend the whole of my time at Hypata?

"Well, I'm really bound for Larissa," I replied, "but I'd like to stay here for three or four days, if I may."

I was purposely vague about the length of my stay, because I was determined not to leave until I had met one of the local witches and seen her do something spectacular, like turning a human being into a bird or a stone. With this object in view, I set off for a walk round the town. Needless to say, I had no idea where to begin my search, so I just started walking and hoped for the best.

I had not gone far before I saw a lady who showed signs of recognizing me. She was young, and to judge by her clothes and jewellery, and the number of servants with her, fairly rich.

"Why, fancy meeting you here!" she exclaimed, as soon as I came up to her.

"Fancy meeting you!" I echoed politely.

"Let me introduce myself," she went on. "My name's Abroia. You must have heard your mother speak of me – I'm one of her oldest friends, and I love all her children as dearly as if they were my own – so why don't you come and stay at my house?"

"Thanks very much," I answered, "but I don't like to desert my present host. He's been very nice to me, and I've no excuse for leaving him. But in spirit, my dear lady, I'm staying with you already!"

"And where are you staying in the flesh?" she asked.

"With a man called Hipparchus."

"What, that stingy old thing?"

"Oh, you mustn't say that," I protested. "He's been quite lavish in his hospitality – in fact, some people might call it positively extravagant."

Abroia smiled, then took me by the hand and drew me aside.

"Whatever you do," she whispered, "watch out for that wife of his. She's a dangerous witch, and a sex fiend into the bargain. She makes eyes at every young man she meets, and if they fail to respond she punishes them by magic. She's turned several of them into animals already, and killed one or two outright. Now, you're a handsome lad, just the sort that any woman might take a fancy to – and you're a stranger here, so no one's going to worry if you suddenly disappear!"

The moment I heard that the object of my long search was actually living under the same roof with me, I lost all interest in Abroia. I got away from her as soon as I could, and hurried back to the house, lecturing myself as follows:

"Now look here, you're always saying you want to see some magic. Well, here's your chance – what are you going to do about it? You'd better not start anything with the woman herself – after all, her husband's a friend of yours, quite apart from being your host. But what about that maid, Palaestra? Palaestra means a wrestling school, doesn't it? Well, why not strip and try a fall with her? I bet if you get a good grip and roll her about a bit, you'll soon find out all you want to know. Servants are generally well acquainted with their employers' secrets."

Hipparchus and his wife were both out when I got to the house, but Palaestra was busy cooking dinner over the fire, so I set to work at once.

"What a pretty girl you are, Palaestra!" I began. "And how charmingly you waggle your hips as you stir that saucepan! I can't help moving mine in sympathy – and I'd give anything for a lucky dip in that saucepan of yours!"

Fortunately she was not at all shy, and she played up splendidly.

"You'd better be careful, young man," she replied. "If you've got any sense or any instinct of self-preservation, you'll keep well away from it. I warn you it's very hot stuff, and if you touch it you'll get badly burnt. When that happens, it won't be any good going to a doctor, for no one will be able to cure you except me. And the trouble about my treatment is that it's rather painful and definitely habit-forming – once you've had it, you'll never be able to get along without it. No matter what I do, you'll always be coming back for another dose of my bittersweet medicine. It's no laughing matter, I assure you. I happen to be a very good cook, and I don't confine my operations to the sort of meat I've got here – I also know how to deal with a fine big carcass like yours. I know how to slaughter it, and skin it, and chop it up into little pieces – delicious! But the part I enjoy most of all is the heart!"

"You're absolutely right," I said. "Why, even at this range you've set my heart on fire. You've started roasting it in the radiant heat that comes out of your eyes – before I've even touched you! So for God's sake give me a dose of that bittersweet medicine you spoke of. My carcass is entirely at your disposal – go ahead and do what you like with it."

Palaestra chuckled contentedly, and from that moment she was mine for the asking. In fact, she promised to come to my room as soon as her master and mistress had gone to bed.

When Hipparchus finally turned up, we all had baths and then sat down to dinner. After the meal, we went on talking over our wine until at last I pretended to be sleepy and retired to my room, where I found that Palaestra had arranged things very efficiently in advance. My servant's bed had been put outside the door, and replaced by a table with a couple of wineglasses on it. There was also a bottle of wine, and plenty of hot and cold water. The whole room was a positive bower of roses, some scattered about on the bedclothes and some festooned round the walls. In fact, the party was all ready to begin as soon as my guest arrived, so I settled down to wait for her.

The moment she had seen her mistress into bed, Palaestra hurried along to join me, and we spent a very pleasant half-hour kissing and drinking one another's health. When we had finally drunk ourselves into a suitable mood for the real business of the night, she addressed me sternly as follows:

"Now remember, young man, I'm not called Palaestra for nothing. You're here to do some wrestling. Now's the time to show your mettle and give a demonstration of your technique."

"Don't you worry," I replied. "You won't catch me backing out. I'm quite prepared to be put to the test, so let's strip and try a fall right away."

"Well, this is what I suggest," she said. "I'll be the trainer and sing out the instructions, and you must be ready to do whatever I say."

"Fire away then," I answered. "You'll find me a very apt pupil."

So she took off all her clothes and instructed me as follows:

"All right, my boy, strip and rub yourself with some of this perfume. Now come to grips with your opponent. Seize him by the legs and throw him down on his back. Now get on top of him and force his legs apart. Work them up and down a few times and then go into a clinch. Now push him off and pummel him all over until you get in under his guard. That's it – don't weaken! Now pull away and make a frontal attack with your teeth. Then once more into the breach – one big push – and the moment you find the enemy giving ground, jump at him and clamp your arms round his waist. Then try not to hurry – wait a bit before you make the final assault. That's all – now you can stop."

I had no difficulty in carrying out her instructions, and when we had finished, I burst out laughing and said:

"Well, sir, I hope you're satisfied with my performance. What's the next item on the programme? Please don't expect me to do anything that's not in the book of rules."

"What nonsense! Of course I won't," said Palaestra, and boxed my ears. "And mind you don't try any tricks of your own, or you'll get into serious trouble."

With these words, she got up and started tidying herself. After a while she came back and knelt down on the bed.

"And now," she said, "let's see if you've enough stamina to do the hip throw. Come on, if you call yourself a wrestler, have a try. That's right, now you've got your opponent on the hip, so give a jerk and press home your advantage. He's at your mercy – make the most of it. The first thing to do is to get a good grip on him. Then force him backwards, still holding him firmly and not allowing him any breathing space. As soon as he shows signs of weakening, lift him up and shove him down again. Don't break out of the clinch a moment before I tell you, but keep bending him backwards until you can pull his legs from under him. Then fling him down on his back and do what you like with him. After that you can afford to relax your grip, for your opponent's down and out for a count, and all his limbs have turned to water!"

"Please, teacher," I said, laughing, "can I give the orders now for a change? And will you please do what I say? First of all, get up and sit beside me. Now pour some water over me, and rub me down, and dry me off – and now, for Heaven's sake, put your arms round me and let me go to sleep!"

We had fun and games like this for several nights running, and the special beauty of these wrestling matches was that both sides invariably won. In fact, I enjoyed myself so much that I quite forgot I was supposed to be going to Larissa. But one night I suddenly remembered the original object of the exercise, and said to Palaestra:

"Darling, do let me know next time your mistress is going to do some magic – turning herself into an animal, or anything like that. I've always longed to watch it being done. Or, better still, do some yourself, if you know how to – for then I could watch you doing all kinds of wonderful things. And I'm sure you do know how – in fact, it's quite obvious from my own experience, for women have always called me as hard as nails, and I've never been the slightest bit interested in any woman before, but now I'm completely under your spell. How did you manage that, if not by magic?"

"Don't be so silly," she replied. "Love's much too powerful a thing to be influenced by magic, and anyway I don't know the first thing about it. Why, I've never even learnt to read, and my mistress is terribly secretive about her methods. But if I get a chance, I'll try and let you watch her doing one of her transformations."

Having come to this arrangement, we went to sleep.

A few days later Palaestra told me that her mistress was planning to turn herself into a bird, so that she could fly off and visit her lover.

"Then now's the time," I said, "to show how much you love me. Do help me to satisfy my curiosity at last."

"Don't worry," she said. "I'm going to."

Accordingly, that evening she took me to the door of my hostess's bedroom, and told me to put my eye to the keyhole. I did so, and saw that the woman was undressing. When she had taken off all her clothes, she walked over to the lamp, picked up two pieces of frankincense and holding one of them in the flame muttered some sort of incantation over it. Then she opened a big cupboard, which was full of bottles, and took one of them out. I do not know what was in it, but it looked rather like olive oil. She poured some of it into her hand, and started rubbing herself all over with it, starting at the toenails and working upwards. Then, quite suddenly, she began to sprout feathers. Her nose grew hooked and horny, and she developed all the outward characteristics of a bird. The next moment she was absolutely indistinguishable from an ordinary screech owl, and as soon as she realized that she had got her wings, she uttered a fearful screech and flew out of the window.

At first I simply could not believe my eyes, and thought I must be dreaming, but having finally convinced myself that I was wide awake, I asked Palaestra to let me see if I could do it too. I was curious to know what it felt like to be turned into a bird: did one, for instance, acquire a bird's mentality?

So Palaestra stole softly into the room and fetched me the bottle. I tore off my clothes and rubbed the stuff all over me – but the result was not at all what I intended. A tail shot out behind me, my fingers and toes disappeared and were replaced by four great nails, exactly like hooves, my hands and feet lost all resemblance to human ones, my ears grew long and pointed, and my face swelled up to a monstrous size. I turned round to look at myself, and found that I was nothing more nor less than a donkey.

I could not even tell Palaestra what I thought of her, for my human voice had gone too, and the only way in which I could express my indignation was to bare my lower teeth and give her the sort of look that donkeys use to register disapproval.

"Oh dear, what an awful thing I've done!" she wailed, burying her face in her hands. "I was in such a hurry, and the bottles were all so alike that I must have brought you the wrong one. This obviously isn't meant for growing feathers. But don't worry, it's easily put right. All you've got to do is eat some roses, then you'll be my darling Lucius again. You don't mind being a donkey just for one night, do you, darling? I'll run and get you some roses first thing in the morning, and you'll be perfectly all right the moment you've eaten them."

Throughout this speech she had been tickling my ears and affectionately patting my hide.

Well, admittedly to all appearances I had made an ass of myself, but inside I was still an intelligent human being called Lucius, even if I could not talk. So silently cursing Palaestra for her silly mistake and grinding my teeth with exasperation, I made my way to the place where I knew that my own horse and a real donkey of Hipparchus's were tethered. When they saw me coming, they immediately assumed that I wanted to eat their fodder. Their ears went back and they prepared to fight for their stomachs with their hooves. As soon as I understood what was worrying them, I went and stood well away from the feeding trough, laughing heartily at the idea that I should want to eat oats – but my laugh sounded just like a bray.

"Oh, if only I hadn't been such a busybody!" I thought. "What will happen if a wolf or some other wild beast comes along? This little adventure's liable to end in my being torn to pieces!"

If I had known what was really in store for me, I should have felt even worse.

In the middle of the night, when everybody was comfortably asleep and everything was quiet, I heard a slight noise on the other side of the wall, as though someone was digging through it. Someone was digging through it, and before long the hole was big enough for that someone to get in. The next moment, he had wriggled through the hole, followed by several others, all carrying swords. After tying up Hipparchus and Palaestra and my servant in their respective beds, they proceeded to ransack the house at their leisure, carrying off all the money and clothes and domestic equipment they could lay their hands on. When they had collected everything they wanted, they got hold of me and the other donkey and the horse, and tied their plunder on our backs. Then they started making their getaway along a rough track that led up into the mountains, keeping us on the move, overloaded as we were, by beating us with sticks.

I cannot say what it was like for the other animals, but as far as I was concerned, being unshod, rather skinny and quite unused to it, I found it absolute agony trotting over the sharp stones with a weight like that on top of me. I stumbled repeatedly, but had to keep going because every time I looked like falling down, one of them gave me a whack across the back of my legs with a stick. It was so painful that once or twice I cried, "Oh, God!" But it sounded like an ordinary donkey's bray, for the "Oh" came out with unexpected volume, and the "God" refused to come out at all. However, it did have some effect: it made them hit me all the harder, for fear I advertised their presence by my brays. So in the end I decided that it was better to suffer in silence, and at least enjoy the privilege of not being beaten so often.

By daybreak we had climbed high into the mountains, and they tied up our mouths in case we stopped to graze and spent the whole morning having breakfast instead of getting on with the journey. So for the moment I had no option but to go on being a donkey. However, about midday we came to a house which apparently belonged to some friends of theirs, for they were given a warm welcome and invited in to lunch, while some oats were provided for us animals. The other two tucked in immediately, but although I was terribly hungry, I started looking round for something else to eat, as raw oats were not at all the sort of diet that I was accustomed to.

At the back of the house I soon spotted a garden full of splendid-looking vegetables, with what appeared to be roses growing at the far side of it. Nobody was watching, for the robbers and their friends were busy having lunch indoors, so I trotted round the house and into this garden, partly with the idea of eating some vegetables, and partly in the hope that the roses would turn me back into a human being. Well, the vegetables were all right, and I fairly stuffed myself with lettuces and radishes and parsley, and various other things that can be eaten raw, but the roses turned out not to be the genuine article. They were merely the flowers of a species of wild laurel, commonly known as a rhododendron – and rhododendron makes the worst lunch in the world for either a horse or a donkey, as it is a deadly poison to them.

At this point, the gardener heard me, and seizing a stick came rushing out into the garden. When he saw what havoc I was making among his vegetables, he took the sort of action that you would expect from a rich householder with strong views on the rights of property who catches a burglar on his premises: he gave me a merciless thrashing on my ribs and legs, cut open both my ears and covered my face with bruises.

After a while I could not stand it any longer. I lashed out with my back legs and sent him sprawling among his precious vegetables, and galloped off into the mountains. When he saw me escaping, he shouted to the others to set the dogs on me. There were any number of them, each about the size of a bear, and I knew they were bound to catch me and tear me to pieces, so after galloping about for a bit I decided that my wisest course was to turn round and head for the house. The dogs came towards me, but their owners called them off and tied them up again, after which they proceeded to give me such a savage beating that the pain of it made me sick up all the vegetables I had eaten.

When the time came to continue our journey, they tied the largest and heaviest pieces of stolen property on my back, and off we went again. What with the beating and the weight I had to carry, and the fact that my hooves were practically worn away, I was absolutely at my last gasp, and made up my mind to fall down and refuse to get up again, even if they beat me to death. The advantage of this plan, as I saw it, was that they would be compelled to divide my load between the horse and the other donkey, and leave me to the mercy of the wolves. But some malignant power must have realized my intention and deliberately frustrated it, for at that moment the other donkey, who had probably been thinking along much the same lines, suddenly dropped in his tracks. The robbers tried to make the poor beast get up by beating him with a stick, and when he took no notice of that they attempted to rouse him by grabbing hold of his ears and tail and pulling them as hard as they could. When this had no effect either, they decided that it was a waste of time to go on fussing round a dead donkey when they were supposed to be making a getaway, so after dividing his load between me and the horse, they disposed of my poor companion in misery by hacking off his legs with a sword and pushing him, still breathing, over a precipice.

When I saw my fellow sufferer hurtling down to his death, and realized what would have happened if I had carried out my plan, I thought I had better put up with the pain in my feet and at all costs keep going, for I told myself that I was bound to come across some roses sooner or later, and so be able to recover my human form. I also heard one of the robbers say that there was not much farther to go, and that the next stop would be the end of their journey. This encouraged me to maintain a steady trot, in spite of my enormous load, and before the day was over we had reached the robbers' headquarters.

After unloading their plunder and storing it away, the robbers took us indoors, where an old woman was sitting in front of a blazing fire.

"Why are you sitting there doing nothing?" one of them shouted at her. "Hurry up and get us something to eat."

"It's all ready," she replied. "There's plenty of bread and wine, and I've cooked some meat for you as well."

"That's good," they said, and started undressing in front of the fire. Then they rubbed themselves with oil, and completed their toilet by ladling some warm water out of the copper on the hob and sloshing it over their heads. A few minutes later some other members of the gang turned up with a large haul of gold and silver and clothes and jewellery. After sharing it out between them, they stowed it away, and then performed their ablutions in much the same way as their colleagues had done. Finally, they all settled down to an enormous meal, followed by a great deal of talking and drinking.

The old woman put down some oats for me and the horse, who started gulping them down as quickly as he could, from a very natural fear that I might eat more than my share, but he need not have worried, for whenever the old woman's back was turned I helped myself to bread off the table.

Next morning the robbers went out to work again, all except one young man who was left to help the old woman. I was depressed to find that he was a very efficient jailer. The old woman presented no problem at all, for I could easily have got away without her seeing me, but this young man was very large and fierce-looking, never went anywhere without his sword, and never forgot to lock the door behind him.

Three days later the rest of the gang arrived back about midnight. This time they had not got any gold or silver with them: all they had managed to collect was a very pretty girl, who was crying as if her heart would break. They threw her down on the rushes that covered the floor, told her to cheer up and ordered the old woman to stay indoors and keep an eye on her. The girl refused to have anything to eat or drink, and just went on crying – with the result that I was soon reduced to tears myself, for I was tethered to the feeding trough quite close to her, and I never could bear to see a pretty girl in trouble.

Meanwhile, the robbers were having dinner in the other room. Just before dawn one of the men who had been detailed to watch the roads came rushing in to report that a rich foreigner was driving past in a carriage full of valuable luggage. Immediately they all jumped up and grabbed their weapons, and, after saddling me and the horse, started driving us towards the road. I was so horrified at the prospect of taking part in a hold-up that I began by walking very slowly indeed, but they increased my rate of progress by their usual method – that is to say, by beating me with a stick.

They got to the road in time to hold up the carriage and kill its owner and his servants. Then they loaded us up with the most valuable part of the stolen property, and hid all the rest in the forest. On the way back they made us go so fast that I trod on a sharp stone by mistake and cut myself very painfully on the hoof, with the result that I started limping.

"Why on earth do we keep that donkey?" asked one of the robbers. "It's always falling down. Let's throw it over a cliff, or it will bring us bad luck."

"An excellent idea," said another. "Let's make it a sort of scapegoat for all our crimes."

Everyone else agreed – so I promptly stopped limping and forgot about the pain in my foot, for the fear of death acted as a very powerful anaesthetic.

When we got back to the house, they unloaded the stolen property and stowed it carefully away, after which they sat down and finished their interrupted meal.

The following night they returned to the forest to collect the rest of the plunder.

"There's not much point in taking that wretched donkey," said one of them. "It's quite useless with that cut in its hoof. We can carry some of the stuff ourselves, and the horse can manage the rest."

So off they went, taking the horse with them.

There was a very bright moon that night, and I started thinking to myself:

"You silly ass, what are you waiting for? If you stay here much longer, you'll soon be providing the vultures with an evening meal. Didn't you hear what they're planning to

do? Do you really want to be thrown off a cliff? It's a bright
moonlit night, and they've all gone away. Now's your chance
– unless you'd prefer to be murdered!"

At this point I suddenly realized that I was not even tied up,
for the strap they used for dragging me along was dangling
loose from my neck. Needing no further encouragement, I
promptly made a bolt for the open. When the old woman
saw me escaping, she grabbed hold of my tail and held on
like grim death.

"If I let an old woman like that stop me," I thought, "I'll
deserve all I get."

So I merely continued to go full speed ahead, and dragged
her along behind me. She shouted to her prisoner to come
out and help. The girl came out all right, but when she saw
the old woman attached to my rump like a sort of subsidi-
ary tail, she rose most nobly to the occasion: she vaulted
on to my back and rode away on me. I was so determined
to rescue her and so anxious to get away myself, that I put
on a tremendous spurt, and the old woman was soon left
far behind.

"O God, please help me to escape!" I heard the girl praying.
Then she put her mouth to my ear and whispered:

"You splendid creature, if you can get me safely home,
I'll see that you never have to do any more work as long as
you live – and I'll give you a whole bushel of oats every day
for breakfast!"

Inspired by the thought of saving the girl's life as well as
my own, and thus earning her eternal gratitude, I galloped
along at a fantastic speed, quite unconscious of my damaged
hoof. But just as we got to a place where the road split into
three, we were unlucky enough to meet our enemies return-
ing from the forest. The moonlight enabled them to spot us

a long way off, and recognizing us immediately, they came dashing up to us and seized hold of the strap round my neck.

"My dear young lady!" said one of them. "Where on earth are you off to at this time of night? Aren't you afraid of ghosts? You'd much better come with us. We'll see you safely back home."

With these words, he wrenched my head round and started pulling me back to the house – whereupon I suddenly remembered my bad foot and began to limp.

"Well, isn't that odd?" he said. "Now we've caught you, you suddenly go lame. But you were quite all right a moment ago, when you were trying to get away. You were streaking along like a racehorse then – in fact you were going so fast that you practically took off!"

The point of these remarks was driven home with a stick, and before long I had more than a sore hoof to worry about – I had a very sore leg as well.

When we got back to the house, the first thing we saw was the old woman's body dangling over the edge of a cliff. She had evidently been so frightened – as she had every reason to be – of what her masters would do to her for letting the girl escape, that she had tied a noose round her own neck and hanged herself in advance.

"Very wise of her!" was their only comment. They cut the rope and let her drop out of sight, with the noose still round her neck. Then they took the girl indoors and tied her up, after which they sat down to dinner and discussed the situation over their wine.

"Well, what are we going to do with her?" asked one of them.

"Throw her over the cliff to join the old woman, of course," replied another. "She was trying to rob us of a valuable piece of property, and if we hadn't caught her in time, she'd have reported us to the authorities. Yes, don't you realize, if she'd once got home, she'd have had us all arrested? The whole gang would have been rounded up, and we'd all have been killed. So we simply can't afford to let her get away with it. But perhaps we shouldn't give her such an easy death as falling on the rocks. Let's think of something really slow and painful – some method of torturing her for quite a long time before she dies."

"I've got it!" said someone at last, after various proposals had been considered and turned down. "Now you must admit this is a real stroke of genius. It'll mean sacrificing the donkey, but he's always been too nervous to be very much use to us, and now he's pretending to be lame – and anyway he aided and abetted the girl in her attempt to escape. So let's slit his throat tomorrow morning and rip open his stomach and pull out all the guts. Then we can put our young friend inside him with just her head sticking out, so that she doesn't suffocate immediately. When we've got her comfortable, we can sew up the donkey's stomach, and put them both out for the vultures. I bet they've never had such a tasty dish before. But just think what it'll be like for her! First of all having to take up residence in a dead donkey – then being cooked in a sort of oven on a hot summer's day under the blazing sun – then slowly dying of hunger, and not even being able to suffocate herself – not to speak of the other little inconveniences like the smell of the rotting carcass and the worms crawling all over her. And finally, the vultures will probably eat their way in and start tearing her to pieces while she's still alive, under the impression that she's part of the donkey." Everyone applauded this proposal and appeared to consider it a wonderful inspiration, but I was absolutely horrified. As if it was not bad enough to have my own throat cut, my wretched body was doomed to become the grave of that poor innocent girl! However, just as it was beginning to get light, the filthy creatures were suddenly attacked by a large body of troops, who tied them all up and marched them off for trial before the local magistrate. As it happened, the girl's fiancé was with the soldiers when they made their raid, for he was the one who had reported the location of the robbers' hideout. So he took charge of her, and led her home mounted on my back. The neighbours spotted us a long way off, and rightly interpreting my triumphant brays as a sign that we brought good news, came running out to welcome us and escorted us back to the house.

The girl made a great fuss of me, as well she might, considering what we had been through together and what a horrible fate we had narrowly escaped. She kept her promise and gave me a whole bushel of oats for breakfast, and enough hay to satisfy a camel, but I never cursed Palaestra so heartily as I did then for not turning me into a dog instead of a donkey – for the dogs were allowed to go into the kitchen and gobble up all the delicious things that were left over from the wedding breakfast.

A few days after the wedding, my mistress told her father that she was very grateful to me and wanted to give me some suitable reward for my services, so he suggested that I should be turned out to grass with the mares.

"Then he'll be completely his own master," he explained, "and have a fine old time making love to the ladies."

It sounded just the sort of thing that a donkey would like, so he sent for one of his grooms and handed me over to him. Delighted at the prospect of having no more heavy weights to carry, I cheerfully allowed the groom to introduce me to a herd of mares, and followed them out into the fields.

But apparently I am the type of person that never has any luck, for the groom soon handed me over to his wife, who set me to work grinding wheat and barley in her mill. Well, that would not have been so bad in itself: no reasonable donkey objects to making himself useful about the house. But the charming lady started hiring me out for the same purpose to all her neighbours – and there were quite a lot of them – in return for a proportion of the flour. As for the daily ration of oats that I had been promised, she used to roast them in the oven, put them in the mill for me to grind and then bake them into oatcakes which she gobbled up herself. All I had to eat was bran.

On the rare occasions when I was turned out to graze with the mares, I got into fearful trouble with the stallions, who suspected me of making passes at their wives. They were always chasing me about and lashing out at me with their hooves – in fact, their jealous horseplay soon made life quite intolerable. The result was that I got very thin and out of condition, for most of the time I was slogging away at the mill, and the rest of it I was being persecuted by the stallions. Either way it was not much fun.

On top of all that, I was often sent up into the mountains to bring down bundles of firewood. This was quite my least favourite occupation, for it meant climbing up an almost vertical mountainside, and with my unshod hooves I found the stony surface peculiarly painful. Worst of all, I had a beastly little boy to drive me, who thought up some new form of cruelty every time we went. To begin with, he used to beat me, even when I was trotting along as fast as I could go, not with an ordinary stick, but with a bundle of sharp twigs; and he always used to beat me on the same part of my leg, so that he very soon laid it open – but he still went on beating me on the sore place.

Then he used to load me up with enough wood to break the back of an elephant, and make me run down the steep slope with it, beating me incessantly. If he noticed my load slipping over to one side, he never did the sensible thing, which would have been to transfer some sticks from the heavier side to the lighter, and so restore the balance. Instead, he would pick up some of the heavy stones that were scattered about on the ground and tie them on to the side that was riding upwards – as if it was not bad enough having to carry all that wood, without carrying a load of useless stones as well. On the way there and back we had to cross a stream, so to save wetting his shoes he used to clamber on to my back and sit there behind the firewood until we were safely over. But what was really unbearable was the way he treated me when I collapsed from sheer exhaustion under the weight of my load. Instead of getting off and helping me up, and if necessary reducing my load, he just sat there and started hitting me all over from my head and ears to my tail, until I somehow scrambled to my feet. Then there was another intolerably cruel trick that he used to play on me. He would collect a bundle of sharp thistles and tie them on to my tail, so that every time I moved they banged against my legs and pricked them all over. There was absolutely no escape, for they were firmly attached to my person, and wherever I went, they came too. If I tried going slowly to minimize the effect of the thistles, he thrashed me with his stick: if I tried going faster to avoid the stick, I suffered all the more from the instrument of torture at my rear. In short, that boy's one object in life was apparently to kill me.

Once, when he had been treating me even worse than usual, I lost my temper and kicked him. He never forgot that kick. A few days later he was told to move some flax from one part of the estate to another, so he got hold of me and tied the flax on to my back – or rather, he tied me to the flax, so that I could not possibly get away from it, for he was planning a really diabolical revenge.

Just as we were starting off, he surreptitiously picked up a piece of burning wood from the fire, and when we were well away from the house applied it to the flax. Naturally it flared up at once, and the next moment I was carrying a bonfire on my back.

Realizing that it was only a matter of seconds before I was roasted alive, I made a dash for the nearest puddle in the road and threw myself down in the wettest part of it, where I twisted and turned and rolled about in the mud, until I had put out the flames. After that I was able to continue my journey in comparative safety and comfort, for the flax was so plastered with mud that he could not set fire to it again, but when we got back, the barefaced little liar actually pretended that I had done it myself, by passing too close to the fire on our way out.

Having failed in his efforts to burn me alive, the little beast thought up something even worse. Next time he was sent into the mountains to fetch firewood, he collected an enormous load for me to carry and proceeded to sell it to a neighbouring farmer. He then took me home, and to account for the fact that I had nothing on my back, concocted a scandalous story about my goings-on.

"I don't know why we bother to keep this donkey," he said. "He's always been frightfully slow and lazy, and now he's developed a new trick – every time he sees a pretty girl or boy he kicks me over and goes rushing after them as if he'd fallen madly in love with them. Then he starts biting them – I suppose it's his way of kissing – and does his very best to mate with them. He's going to get you into a lot of trouble, for he's always knocking people down and treating them like that, and they're liable to sue you for damages. Why, just now, as we were coming back, he caught sight of a woman going into a field – so he promptly shook off every stick he was carrying, scattered them about all over the place and then threw the woman down in the middle of the road and started trying to mate with her. Luckily there were plenty of people about and they all came running to help me, so we managed to pull him off just in time – otherwise she'd have been torn to pieces by this handsome lover of hers!"

"In that case," said the groom, "you'd better put him down. Give the offal to the dogs, and we'll have the rest cooked for dinner. If anyone asks what's happened to him, you can say he was killed by a wolf."

The little wretch was delighted, and would have cut my throat on the spot, but for the advice of a farmer who happened to be standing by – advice which saved my life, but at a fearful price.

"Oh no, don't do that," he said. "A donkey's always useful for grinding corn and carrying things about, and this particular problem's very easily solved. If you don't want him running after the girls, all you've got to do is neuter him. Then he won't have any more of these troublesome attacks. He'll grow tame and fat, and carry as much as you like without turning a hair. If you don't know how to do it, I'll come back in a day or two and perform the operation myself – and I'll guarantee to make him as gentle as a lamb."

Everyone thought this an excellent idea – everyone, that is, except me, for my eyes filled with tears at the prospect of losing what little manhood I still possessed, and I swore I would never live to be a eunuch. Rather than submit to such an indignity, I made up my mind to starve myself to death or throw myself over a precipice.

However, late that night news came from the village that the young couple to whom we all belonged had been swept away and drowned by a tidal wave while walking along the beach the previous afternoon. So that was the end of them. In the circumstances nobody saw much point in going on being a slave, and after helping themselves to as much of their late master's property as they could carry, all the workers on the estate ran away. The groom loaded me up with all the useful things he could lay his hands on, and set off with me and the mares for Macedonia. Although I was rather annoyed at always having to do the donkey work, I welcomed this new development, for it saved me from being neutered, if nothing else.

It was a very exhausting journey. We travelled night and day, and never stopped until we arrived, three days later, at a large town in Macedonia called Beroea. There our new owners decided to settle down, so they put us up for sale in the marketplace, where a loud-voiced auctioneer advertised our charms, and prospective customers kept opening our mouths and looking at our teeth to see how old we were. Eventually I was the only one that remained unsold, and the auctioneer told my master to take me away again.

"As you see, I've managed to sell all the others," he said, "but I can't do anything with this one."

Just then, however, Fate did one of her famous about-turns, and produced a new master for me, though not at all the type of master that I should have chosen. He was an old pervert belonging to the curious sect which worships Atargatis – that is, if you can call it worshipping when you turn your goddess into a sort of tramp and make her go from village to village begging. I was sold to this gentleman for the princely sum of thirty drachmas, and off I had to go with him, feeling very sorry for myself.

When we got to his lodgings, Philebus – for that was his name – stopped outside the door and shouted:

"Darlings, I've bought you the most heavenly slave! He's ever so strong and handsome, and he comes all the way from Cappadocia!"

The darlings, who were his fellow perverts, all clapped their hands delightedly, thinking that his purchase was human, but when they saw that I was only a donkey, they started being very witty at his expense.

"My dear!" they screamed. "Wherever did you get that from? It's not a slave at all, it's your new boyfriend! Have a wonderful time, darling – and lots of lovely little foals just like their father!"

Next morning, however, they got down to some serious work – at least that is what they called it. Having dressed their goddess in her smartest clothes, they put her on my back, and off we went for a tour of the countryside. Whenever we came to a village, I, with my load of divinity, was made to stand still, and the musician of the party struck up an inspired little melody on his flute – whereupon the others took off their veils and started rolling their heads from side to side, gashing their arms with knives and sticking out their tongues and cutting them, until the whole place was fairly dripping with their innocent blood. The first time I saw it I trembled violently, for fear the goddess should develop a taste for donkey blood as well as human.

When they had finished hacking themselves to pieces, they sent a collection plate round the circle of spectators and got it back piled high with obols and drachmas. Occasionally someone would give them some dried figs, or some cheese, or a bottle of wine, or a bushel of corn – or some oats for the donkey. So they managed to live quite comfortably on the proceeds of their piety, and were always making thank-offerings to the goddess on my back.

At one of the villages we came to, they made a convert of a handsome young fellow who lived there, and took him back to their lodgings where they proceeded to make use of him in their own peculiar way. Up to then I had always kept my opinions to myself, but this was really too much for me, and I let out a shocked "Good God!" Unfortunately it did not sound quite like that: it sounded like a loud donkey's bray.

Now, as it happened, one of the villagers had lost his donkey, and a search party was passing the house at that very moment. Hearing my exclamation, they naturally assumed that I was the missing animal, so they marched straight into the house without knocking and caught my masters in the act. The spectacle sent them into fits of laughter and they ran off to tell the rest of the village how the holy men employed their spare time. My masters were so embarrassed at being found out that they left the village the same night.

When we got to a lonely bit of road, they started cursing and swearing at me for betraying their mysteries. Well, I should not have minded that, for I was quite used to being insulted, but I minded very much what they did next, which was to remove the goddess from my back and put her on the ground, strip off all my trappings, tie me to a large tree and flog me practically to death with a cat-o'-nine-tails.

"That'll teach you to keep quiet in future," they said.

They even talked of cutting my throat, which they felt was the very least I deserved for ruining their reputation and seriously reducing their income. The only thing that stopped them was the look of dumb reproach on the goddess's face as she sat there in the middle of the road, deprived of all means of transport.

When they had finished flogging me, they replaced the lady on my back and started off again. Towards evening we came to the house of a rich friend of theirs, who luckily happened to be in. He agreed to put the goddess up for the night, and offered her some sort of sacrifice, but my only vivid memory of the place is that I narrowly escaped being killed there.

One of our host's friends had made him a present of a wild ass's leg, and his chef had carelessly allowed it to be stolen by one of the dogs that were always running in and out of the kitchen. When he found it had disappeared, he was so terrified of what his master might do to him that he decided to hang himself, but his damned busybody of a wife had another suggestion.

"Now don't do anything desperate, darling," she said. "Just do as I tell you, and everything will be perfectly all right. Take this donkey to a place where you won't be seen, and cut its throat. Then chop off a piece of its leg to match the one that's been stolen, bring it back here, pop it in the oven and serve it up for dinner. You can throw the rest of the carcass over a cliff somewhere, and they'll think it's just run away. As a matter of fact, it'll taste much better than the other one – you can see how plump it is."

"What an excellent idea!" said the chef. "However did you think of it? It's obviously the only way out. I'll do it right away."

They were standing quite close to me at the time, and I could see what was coming. It seemed to me only prudent to put as much distance as possible between me and his butcher's cleaver, so I broke the strap that tethered me, kicked up my heels and galloped into the dining room, where I rushed round upsetting all the tables and lamps, while inwardly congratulating myself on my presence of mind – for I assumed that the master of the house would consider me too high-spirited to be left at large, and tell someone to lock me up. However, the only effect of this ingenious manoeuvre was to put me in even deadlier peril, for it convinced them all that I had gone mad, and every man in the room grabbed hold of a sword or a spear or a cudgel and prepared to slaughter me. Realizing the gravity of the situation, I bolted into the room where my masters were going to sleep, and they slammed the door behind me and locked me in.

Early next morning our little company of pious tramps took the road again, with the goddess on my back, and eventually arrived at a large village, where they started

preaching an entirely new point of doctrine, namely that
the goddess should not be lodged in a human dwelling, but
in the temple of the chief local deity. The villagers readily
agreed to billet her on their own goddess, and directed us
to a poorhouse.

After spending several days there, my masters decided to
move on to a nearby town, and asked for their goddess to be
returned. They were given permission to enter the holy pre-
cincts and fetch her out themselves, and having done so they
mounted her on my back and started off. However, under
cover of taking the goddess, they had also helped themselves
to a golden bowl which had been placed in the temple as an
offering. As soon as the villagers discovered the theft, they
came galloping after us on horseback. Having overtaken
us, they jumped down from their horses, seized hold of my
masters and started calling them names and demanding the
return of the stolen property. Everyone was searched, and
the bowl was finally run to earth under the goddess's skirts.
So the holy sisterhood were taken back to the village and
put in prison, the goddess was presented to another temple
and the bowl was restored to its rightful owner.

Next day, the villagers decided to sell all the criminals'
effects, including me, and I was bought by a baker who lived
in the next village. He then proceeded to buy ten bushels of
corn, which he tied onto my back, and I had to carry them
all the way to his house. When we got there, he took me
into his mill, where I saw any number of four-footed fellow
slaves, each turning a separate millstone; the other half of
the building was piled high with sacks of flour. As I was
new to the job and had just come a long way with a heavy
load, he gave me a short rest before setting me to work, but
next morning they tied a piece of cloth over my eyes and

yoked me to the handle of one of the millstones. Then they started trying to make me walk round.

Well, of course I knew perfectly well how to grind corn, having done it only too often before, but I pretended not to understand what was wanted. However, it was no use, for they just stood in a circle round the millstone and hit me, one after another, with their sticks. As I was blindfold, I never knew where the next blow was coming from, and in my efforts to avoid them I was soon spinning round like a top. Thus I learnt from bitter experience that a slave is well advised to use his own initiative, rather than wait for encouragement from his master.

After a few weeks of this I was nothing but skin and bone, so my master decided to sell me. This time I was bought by a market gardener who needed transport to run his business. Every morning he used to load me up with vegetables and take me off to market. Then, as soon as they had been sold, back we would go to the garden, where he would spend the rest of the day digging and planting and watering, while I stood about doing nothing.

It was an absolutely wretched life. For one thing, it was winter by this time, and my master was far too poor to buy any bedding for himself even, let alone for me. Then I was always paddling about in wet mud, or walking barefoot across sharp ridges of frozen soil; and we never had anything to eat but lettuces – and very tough and bitter they were too.

One day, on our way to the garden, we met a gentleman in military uniform who addressed us in Italian and asked the gardener where he was taking that donkey – in other words, me. My master made no reply, presumably because he did not understand the language. The officer was so annoyed at being ignored that he gave the gardener a cut with his cane, whereupon the latter made a dive at his ankles, jerked him off his feet and laid him flat in the road. Having got his opponent down, he started hitting him and kicking him and banging his head very hard on the pavement. At first the officer attempted to fight back, and swore he would draw his sword and kill him the moment he got up.

"You shouldn't have told me that," replied the gardener. "Now I know what to do, don't I?"

With these words, he drew the sword himself, threw it as far away as he could and went on hitting him. Finding that the situation was getting beyond him, the officer shammed dead, which gave the gardener such a fright that he promptly abandoned the supposed corpse, and stopping only to pick up the sword, mounted me and galloped back to the town. Not feeling safe even there, he asked another gardener to look after his business, and went into hiding with me at the house of a friend of his. Well, of course it was easy enough for him to hide in a cupboard, but I presented a somewhat bigger problem, which they finally solved by picking me up by the legs, lugging me up a ladder and locking me in an attic.

Meanwhile, as it later transpired, the officer had struggled to his feet and staggered with aching head back to the town, where he met some of his brother officers and told them about the gardener's outrageous behaviour. They soon found out where we were and sent for the police, who came and banged on the door and said that everyone was to go outside. But when all the visible occupants of the house had been lined up in the street, my master was not among them. So they all started arguing at the tops of their voices, the officers insisting that the gardener and his donkey must be somewhere in the house, and the police retorting angrily that there was no sign of either of them.

Between them they made such a noise in the narrow street that I heard it up in my attic, and as usual my curiosity got the better of me. I poked my head through the window to see what all the shouting was about – and gave the whole show away. The officers spotted me immediately and let out a view halloo, the police made a thorough search of the house, and my master was discovered in his cupboard and haled off to prison to answer for his crime. As for me, I was brought down to earth again and handed over to the officers, who were still roaring with laughter at the way I had betrayed my presence in the attic and thus informed against my own master. In fact, that little faux pas of mine was probably the origin of the modern phrase: "Don't stick your neck out!"

What happened to the gardener after that I have no idea, for the officers decided to sell me, and were lucky enough to get a whole twenty-five drachmas for me. My new owner was the chef of a very rich man from Thessalonica, the capital of Macedonia, and he had a brother who did the baking and pastry-making in the same household. The brothers had always been great friends, and shared a room in which they kept their various implements, all jumbled up together. When I arrived, this room became my stable, but it was also a sort of larder, for every night they used to bring back all the meat and fish and bread and pastry that was left over from their master's dinner and store it away there.

Having provided me with this delightful company, off they went to have a bath, locking the door behind them. Well, naturally I said a long farewell to the oats that they had given me, and started sampling their own exquisite handiwork. It was the first time for ages that I had tasted decent food, and I made the most of it; but I was fairly cautious to begin with, and there was so much of it that for several nights the signs of my gormandize went unnoticed. Finding that they were totally unaware of what was happening, I turned my attention to the special delicacies, and generally let myself go.

Even when they did notice my depredations, their first reaction was to suspect one another, so they merely made a few pointed remarks about people who misappropriated public property, and resolved to be more careful in future about their stock-taking. In the mean time, I continued to live on the fat of the land, with the result that I soon recovered my good looks, and my coat became sleek and glossy.

Eventually the honest fellows noticed the discrepancy between my excellent condition and my undiminished pile of oats, which gave them an inkling of the truth. So the next time they went out, they shut the door behind them as usual, but instead of going away they put their eyes to the keyhole and watched me having dinner.

The sight of a donkey eating his way through such an incredible menu sent them into fits of laughter, and they called all the other servants to see it too, and they burst out laughing as well. Between them they made so much noise that their master heard it in the dining room, and asked what the joke was. When they told him, he got up from the table and applied his eye to the keyhole just in time to see me setting to work on a large helping of wild boar, at which he let out a shriek of merriment and came bursting into the room.

I was dreadfully embarrassed at being found out, for I feared he would think me a glutton as well as a thief, but he was so amused that he took me straight into the dining room and ordered a special table to be laid for me. This was then loaded with food, of a type that would be quite unsuitable for an ordinary donkey, such as soup, fish, meat and oysters, with every conceivable dressing from mustard and olive oil to caviar. As a matter of fact, I was full up already, but finding that my luck had turned at last, I thought my only hope was to enter into the spirit of the thing, so I went up to the table and ate a hearty meal.

Everyone rocked with laughter, and eventually somebody said:

"I bet that donkey wouldn't say no to a glass of wine, if you poured it out for him!"

"Let's try and see," said my host (whose name, by the way, was Menecles), so his butler filled a glass for me, and I was only too happy to drink it.

Menecles was now convinced, as well he might be, that I was a most unusual animal. He therefore instructed his secretary to give the chef twice as much as he had paid for me, and told a young freedman of his to teach me as many amusing tricks as he could. He could hardly have had an easier job, for I was an extremely apt pupil. First of all he taught me to lie on a couch, propped up on one elbow like a human being. Then he taught me to wrestle with him and dance on my hind legs. Finally, he taught me to nod and shake my head in answer to questions, and do various other things that I was perfectly capable of doing already.

Before long I was quite a celebrity, and everyone was talking about the wonderful donkey that wrestled and danced and drank its master's wine, but my two greatest accomplishments were answering questions by nodding or shaking my head, and catching the butler's eye when I wanted a drink. Of course, if they had known I was really a human being, they would have thought nothing of it, but luckily I was in a position to turn their ignorance to my advantage.

Besides all my other tricks, I learnt to carry my master at a very slow walking pace, and also to trot so smoothly that he could hardly tell I was doing it. In return for this, I was given some very expensive purple trappings, a bridle ornamented with silver and gold, and a harness with bells all over it, so that I had music wherever I went.

I said that Menecles came from Thessalonica, but I have not yet explained what he was doing in this part of Macedonia. The answer is that he had come to collect some gladiators for a show that he was putting on, and as soon as he had got enough he started home again. We set off early in the morning, and whenever the road was too bumpy for him to be comfortable in his carriage, I had to carry him on my back.

Eventually we reached our destination, to find that my fame had travelled ahead of me, and everyone was dying to see the donkey that did such wonderful tricks, and wrestled and danced just like a human being. However, I had to disappoint my public, for my master preferred to exhibit me at a series of private views to which only the most important people were invited, and to use me as a floor show at his more exclusive dinner parties.

My trainer followed suit, and converted me into a valuable source of income by locking me up in a room and charging my fans an exorbitant fee for admission. In spite of this, I had any number of visitors, and they all brought me something to eat. It was usually the type of thing that would be bound to disagree with a donkey, but I made it my policy never to refuse anything, with the result that I soon grew immensely fat.

One of my visitors was a foreign girl, who was very rich and not at all bad to look at. The moment she saw me having lunch, she fell passionately in love with me. I suppose it was partly because of my exquisite beauty, and partly because I seemed so human in other respects that she could not help wondering what I should be like in bed. Anyhow, she had a word with my trainer and offered him a large sum of money if he would let her spend the night with me. Well, obviously he could not have cared less whether the experiment was successful or not, so he took the money and agreed to do what she asked.

Sure enough, when my master had finished with me in the dining room and sent me off to bed, I found the lady waiting for me. She had had a mattress put on the floor, complete with plenty of soft pillows, and there she was lying on it. As soon as I arrived, she told her maid to go and sleep in the corridor, and after taking off all her clothes and turning up the lamp as high as she could, she stood beside it and rubbed herself all over with perfume from an alabaster bottle. Then she rubbed some on me, especially round my nostrils, after which she gave me a kiss, and murmuring the sort of endearments that women go in for on these occasions, got hold of my halter and started pulling me gently towards the bed.

I cannot say I needed much pulling, for I had drunk a lot of wine that night at dinner, the perfume had a most stimulating effect, and the girl, now I came to look at her, was extremely attractive. So I lay down on the bed, but I was very uncertain what to do next, for my donkey career up to date had been one of complete celibacy, and I was terribly afraid I might do her a serious injury, or even be had up for murder. However, I need not have worried, for finding that I was not uninterested she started kissing me in the most seductive way, and finally lay down beside me and arranged things to my entire satisfaction.

Even then I was so nervous that I tried to back away, but she hung on to me and would not let me go. Realizing at last that I was necessary to her happiness, I stopped worrying and put myself completely at her disposal.

"After all," I thought, "I can't be any worse than Pasiphae's boyfriend."

As a matter of fact, she was so enthusiastic that she kept me hard at it all night.

In the morning she got up and went away, but not before she had arranged to spend another night with me on the same terms. Needless to say, my trainer was only too glad to cooperate, for not only was he getting all the pay while I did all the work, but it also meant a new trick to show his master. So he shut us up together several nights running, and she practically wore me out. Then one night he told my master about my latest accomplishment, pretending that he had taught me it himself, and Menecles came and peeped through the keyhole while I was being put through my paces. He was so delighted with the spectacle that he made up his mind to reproduce it in public.

"Don't say a word to anyone," he told my trainer, "and on the day of the show we'll put him in the middle of the arena with some female convict or other, and let him do it in front of the whole audience!"

So they got hold of a girl who would otherwise have been thrown to the lions, and told her to go into my room and start stroking me.

Finally, when the day came for my master to display his public spirit, I was the star turn on the programme. I made my entrance as follows: the girl and I lay down side by side on a huge double bed constructed of Indian tortoiseshell reinforced with gold, which was then put on a sort of trolley and wheeled into the middle of the arena, where we were greeted by a great round of applause. Then a table was put beside us and loaded with all the ingredients of a really first-class dinner, while a couple of good-looking slaves came and stood at our elbows, ready to fill our glasses from a pair of golden decanters.

When everything was ready, my trainer, who was standing just behind me, told me to start eating; but I did not feel much like it, for I found it most embarrassing lying there in the middle of the circus, and I was terribly afraid that a lion or a bear might suddenly leap out at me. Just then, however, an attendant walked past carrying a large bunch of flowers, among which I spotted the yellow petals of some roses.

I instantly jumped off the bed. Everyone took it for granted that I was going to do some of my famous dancing, but instead of that I galloped after the attendant and started tearing out the roses from his bouquet and gobbling them up. While the audience were still gaping in astonishment, my animal appearance suddenly fell away, the donkey became a thing of the past and the real Lucius stood there naked before them.

This unrehearsed transformation scene naturally created a tremendous sensation, and the circus was divided into two schools of thought, those who wanted me burnt at the stake immediately for practising black magic, and those who preferred to delay sentence until they had heard what I had to say for myself. Luckily, the governor of the province happened to be in the audience, so I ran over to his box and shouted up at him that I had been turned into a donkey by a witch's maid in Thessaly.

"Please put me in custody," I went on, "until I've satisfied you that I'm speaking the truth."

"Well, tell me your name, to start with," said the Governor, "and the names of your parents and relations, if you claim to have any, and the name of the place where you were born."

So I told him my father's name in full, and then continued:

"And my first name is Lucius, and my brother's is Caius, and our surnames are the same as my father's. I write short stories and various other things, and my brother writes poetry – he's particularly good at elegiacs. And we all come from Patrae in Achaea."

"In that case," said the Governor, "your father is one of my oldest friends. He's often had me to stay, and shown me every possible kindness. If you're his son, I'm quite sure you wouldn't lie to me."

With these words he jumped up from his chair, threw his arms round my neck and kissed me, and finally took me home with him.

Soon afterwards my brother arrived with money and clothes and everything else I needed, and there was a public hearing of my case, at which I was formally acquitted of all charges against me. When it was all over, my brother and I strolled down to the harbour, and having found a ship to take us home, arranged for our luggage to be carried on board.

Before we left, however, I thought I had better pay a call on the girl who had fallen in love with me when I was a donkey, for I hoped she would find me even more attractive as a human being. She seemed delighted to see me, though I suppose it was really my news value that appealed to her, and asked me to have dinner and spend the night with her. I accepted her invitation, for I felt it would be asking for trouble to turn down an old admirer from my donkey days just because I had gone up in the world since then. So I had dinner with her, and put on a lot of her scent, and made myself a crown of roses, which were now, needless to say, my favourite flowers.

Finally, when it was time to go to bed, I jumped up and, with the idea of giving her a treat, took off all my clothes and displayed myself in the nude, fondly imagining that compared with a donkey I should be quite irresistible. But she was so disappointed to find that I was in every respect a normal human being that she actually spat in my face.

"Get the hell out of my house!" she screamed. "Go and sleep somewhere else!"

"Why, what on earth have I done?" I asked.

"Oh, for God's sake, don't you understand?" she exclaimed. "It was the donkey I fell in love with, not you! And I did so hope that there'd be one thing left, at least, to remind me of that splendid great animal – but just look at you – you're nothing but a wretched little monkey!"

She then called her servants and told them to throw me out of the house. So, with the crown of roses still on my head, my perfumed body was dumped naked on the naked bosom of the earth, in whose cold embrace I spent the rest of the night.

Early next morning I ran back to the ship to put some clothes on, and told my brother about my ridiculous adventure. Soon afterwards we set sail with a brisk wind behind us, and a few days later arrived at Patrae, where I made a thank-offering to the gods for bringing me safe home at last, after leading me a dog's, or rather a donkey's, life for so long.

ALMA CLASSICS

ALMA CLASSICS aims to publish mainstream and lesser-known European classics in an innovative and striking way, while employing the highest editorial and production standards. By way of a unique approach the range offers much more, both visually and textually, than readers have come to expect from contemporary classics publishing.

LATEST TITLES PUBLISHED BY ALMA CLASSICS

www.almaclassics.com

Gustave Flaubert	*Madame Bovary*
Ford Madox Ford	*The Good Soldier*
J.W. von Goethe	*The Sorrows of Young Werther*
Nikolai Gogol	*Petersburg Tales*
Thomas Hardy	*Tess of the d'Urbervilles*
Nathaniel Hawthorne	*The Scarlet Letter*
Henry James	*The Portrait of a Lady*
Franz Kafka	*The Metamorphosis and Other Stories*
D.H. Lawrence	*Lady Chatterley's Lover*
Mikhail Lermontov	*A Hero of Our Time*
Niccolò Machiavelli	*The Prince*
Edgar Allan Poe	*Tales of Horror*
Alexander Pushkin	*Eugene Onegin*
William Shakespeare	*Sonnets*
Mary Shelley	*Frankenstein*
Robert L. Stevenson	*Strange Case of Dr Jekyll and Mr Hyde and Other Stories*
Jonathan Swift	*Gulliver's Travels*
Antal Szerb	*Journey by Moonlight*
Leo Tolstoy	*Anna Karenina*
Ivan Turgenev	*Fathers and Children*
Mark Twain	*Adventures of Huckleberry Finn*
	The Adventures of Tom Sawyer
Oscar Wilde	*The Picture of Dorian Gray*
Virginia Woolf	*Mrs Dalloway*
Stefan Zweig	*A Game of Chess and Other Stories*

**Order online for a 20% discount at
www.almaclassics.com**